A King's Ransom

The Second novel in the

Blood of a Queen trilogy

A Novel

TOI POWELL

The TOI House | New Jersey

A King's Ransom: The second novel in the
Blood of a Queen **trilogy.**

ISBN-10: 0-9975973-2-1
ISBN-13: 978-0-9975973-2-5

Book cover design by Toi Powell

ToiPowell.com

Download the Soundtrack

BLOOD OF A QUEEN

Performed by Toi Powell
Available at the following locations:
iTunes, Apple Music, Google Play,
Amazon mp3, Tidal, Spotify

Each one of us possess the formidable power of love. In the face of adversity, use it with everything you've got.

A King's Ransom

The Second novel in the
Blood of a Queen trilogy

A Novel

TOI POWELL

Chapter 1

The voices of Pieces who haven't seen each other for quite some time echo loudly throughout the empty building. Sean sits on a nearby bench press waiting for Scully to enter, but he's taking forever. Sean wonders how long he'd have to wait before this impromptu meeting begins. Being in the company of these men, makes him "uneasy". He stiffens up and hardens his expression each time a set of curious eyes lands on him for longer than a second.

"Why's he here?"

"That's that stupid kid with the book, aint it?"

"He's a cocky little prick, I bet he sucks a good…"

Sean stands. The men are suddenly amused. He can probably take them on one by one, he thinks. They're old, fat and probably haven't squared up in years. That's what they have security for, but security has to wait outside. It's just him and the old dudes. Yeah, he can take em.

He squeezes his fists.

This is my gym! This is my house.

The Pieces are no longer amused. Sean's audacity fuels their temper as he prepares to confront them.

"This new kid needs to be taught some manners."

"I'm no kid. But you're welcome to find out if you

don't believe me," Sean replies.

"How 'bout I *don't* believe you." One of Scully's oldest Pieces takes a step towards Sean, knuckles cracking, suspenders dangling along each hip. He unbuttons his top button, then the next, and then the next.

Sean takes off his jacket, unafraid, waiting to see what he's made of. This Piece is twice his size, solid like Scully yet short and stocky. He can probably pack a heavy punch, a devastating blow if Sean isn't careful. It's been awhile since he's trained at the gym, but Sean looks down.

"Church shoes?" he asks.

"These aint church shoes. They're…"

"They're church shoes," Sean finishes. *Yeah, I can take him.*

The other Pieces remain seated laughing heartily, urging the man to leave the kid alone.

"No! If Scully wants to bring in new blood, he's gonna have to teach him some respect. And if he won't, I will!" He unbuckles his belt and slides it out of the loop of his trousers.

"So, you gonna spank me with that or…what? What do you plan on doing with that old man?" Sean asks, not sure whether to attack or laugh.

"Let me show you," he growls. In an instant the man charges towards Sean. Surprisingly, he's quick and light on his feet.

Sean grounds himself, bracing for impact just as Scully enters the room. He's followed by Jim, the old man who manages the gym. Jim takes a seat away from everyone else, pulls out his old carving knife and whittles away at a piece of wood.

"So, what's this I hear about Scully *needing* to teach this new blood some respect?"

Everyone in the room freezes, including Sean and his hot-tempered Piece.

"I meant no disrespect Scully. I was only saying that this kid…"

"You were only saying *nothing*."

The Pieces glance at each other, silently unwilling to come to the defense of their fellow Piece.

"I do what I do for a reason," Scully continues. "I don't need to explain, articulate, write down or announce a thing to any of you, unless I want to. *Sean*, not kid, works for me. He answers to me. I know that's not how we traditionally do things around here, but this is how *I* do things. You have a problem with him, you come to me. *Directly* to me. You want to lay your hands on someone, you want to pull off your belt…?"

"Scully, I…"

"Shut up! You tried to humiliate someone under my care. You tried to attack someone under my protection. Was I not clear on who he was when he came to your house to collect your dues?"

"Yes, you were."

Scully looks around the room, still unsatisfied.

"Yes." The rest of the men join in.

"The same way I demand you respect each other, and myself is the same respect you will have for Sean. Have I made myself clear?"

The men nod.

Sean is shocked and impressed. A smile begins to curl on his lips until Scully's eyes find him.

"And you..." Scully's eyes are fierce, lit with fire and heat.

Sean's heart stops.

"You still have training to do and we'll get there. But...if you ever pull this crap again and bring us to the brink of disarray, violence and war within the ranks, you won't have to worry about no damn belt. I'll deal with you myself. Now, sit the hell down!"

Sean can't remember if his butt hit the seat before or after Scully finished speaking. War? He hadn't thought of that. Thinking back, he can see how civil these men are with each other, but not because they want to be, but because they *have* to be. The slightest disagreement could cause all-out war between the districts! That would be bad, not only for Scully, but for the innocent people who actually live in those districts. Overwhelming regret settles over him.

Scully pulls a chair towards the center of the room. The men fall silent, waiting for him to speak. He waits until every man is seated before he takes his. Still, they say nothing.

Scully is tired. He's worn out. It's rare for him to appear so vulnerable in front of his men, but things have been changing lately.

"There was a time in my life when I knew nothing but pain, emptiness and sadness. I used to think that by being this...I would be something better, someone more important. But, I now realize that by *being this,* I'm *still* nothing. I thought I wanted this life. Actually...," he corrects himself, "...I *knew* I wanted this life, but what I didn't grasp at the time, is that everything I wanted would come at a tremendous price."

His men stir in their seats while Sean moves closer to the group, suddenly intrigued, defeated in his thoughts.

"A man is nothing without family," he continues. "He's nothing if no one *needs* him. A man without family is like a lung without oxygen. He's useless, unnecessary."

He takes a deep breath. "I thought by making a million dollars, I could make two, and if I made two, I could make four. But what good is four million dollars if you have no one to share it with?"

For some of the Pieces, it's unbearable to watch. Expressing emotions in this business is taboo. Others avoid eye contact with him altogether, but only one of them is stoic as stone. Sean on the other hand can't turn away. He respects Scully's honesty. To him, this is what makes Scully, the KingPin. That he can be vulnerable with his men, and still put the fear of God in them if they dared betray him. But he's more than a KingPin. He's a man. A man whose clawed his way out of the monster he used to be and into a man who's beginning to realize his mistakes and prays it's not too late.

"Simply put, I made a few difficult decisions several years ago and it's finally catching up with me. Someone attempted to assassinate me and my friends, back then. An amazing woman and mother was killed that night...because of me." His voice shakes. "There was no reason for her to die. Tony, you remember that night?"

Tony nods.

"That same night, I also sacrificed my queen."

Instantly, the men become even more somber. They fully understand how much of a difficult, yet a powerful chess strategy this is. If done successfully, it changes the game and you fight ahead with nothing left to lose. Judging by Scully's track record, he executed it with great success. Although it was the most important and pivotal moment of his budding career, it was also the hardest, most painful thing he'd ever done.

"Someone tried to kill *us!* We had two beautiful, innocent little girls with us, and they tried to…" the memory flashes before him like a nightmare. He shakes it out of mind.

"…but they couldn't. I made sure of that. What kills me is that we never found who was responsible, and I know he's still out there, waiting. Waiting for an opportunity to strike again. It's been years since then, but I never let my guard down and I don't plan to now."

Scully gathers himself and straightens his suit jacket.

"One of the young girls has gone missing. She's out here, in New York and we need to find her before they do. I need surveillance in every borough and district, now. If we find her, no one is approach her. You hit me up, and I'll take it from there."

Scully presses a few buttons on his phone and within seconds, every man in the room reaches for his. Out of curiosity, Sean tries to peek over the shoulder of a Piece until, his phone vibrates like the others.

Sean touches the screen to open an image file. He looks as if he's seen a ghost.

"Everyone," says Scully, "Take a good look at this picture. This young lady is my beautiful daughter, Ruby."

****

The men shake hands and solemnly promise to do Scully the favor he's asked of them. Once Scully's confirmed their loyalty and commitment, he reverts to his old self in a matter of seconds. Strength emanates from him yet again and all seems to be well as each Piece is given a handshake and a brick of thousand dollar bills for their time and trouble.

Sean's heading out when Scully abruptly shuts the door behind the last person ahead of him.

"Hold on, son. I wanna speak to you."

Sean steps back and waits.

This isn't good. What the hell is going on? Ruby's dad?! Her real dad? But he can't possibly know that I know Ruby, right? Maybe he's pissed I challenged the Pieces in his safe space. Yeah, he's pissed about that. God, I hope he's only pissed about that.

The last Piece to leave decides to wait patiently on the other side of the door. The others drive off, but he stays to listen, desperately straining to hear a conversation that neither he nor his counterparts are trusted enough to witness.

Something's very strange about all of this. Very strange indeed. What's so special about this kid? he thinks.

This kid don't know about hustling, nor does he have the stomach for it. I could tell the moment he came to collect earnings, he's weak! There's nothing special about him, yet Scully keeps dragging him around like a damn pet!

I can't stand seeing that little coward collecting my profits like he runs things around here. I'm a Piece for God's sake! He's nothing! But, Scully's having a private meeting with him. Why?

"Sean, I'm trusting this special task to you, because you don't want anything from me but an opportunity and a new start in life, and that's what I respect about you. I trust you, more than my own men. The others are corrupt; they'll look for an opportunity to come up while pretending to help me."

"Then why'd you show them her picture? Why involve them at all?" Sean asks.

"Because they have the bodies and the numbers. I need as many boots on the ground as quickly as possible. This is my army and I'm mobilizing them to find my daughter."

"You have to pay them to do that?"

"No one does anything in this world for free, Sean. The sooner you realize that, you can get ahead of it. If you have the means, give them what they expect so you get what you need. The more you fight against it, the more time, money and resources you waste. Think more than 5 steps ahead. How will you get the best results for what you want? You need to incentivize and if you address what they want and need beforehand, you don't give them a chance to ask. Because once they ask, they have negotiating power and if that happens, you're in a fight to retain yours. Never place yourself in a position where you have to fight to retain your power. But if you have to, know how."

Sean listens. Although Scully sounds a little preachy, this business is his church and this philosophy is his religion. Sure, he can punch holes in it, but why? No one has been able to bring this man and his empire to its knees in over 20 years. His strategic thinking has kept him and his men alive and flourishing all of this time. Perhaps he should stop questioning his methods and let him speak.

"I see you as a son, Sean. In this short time I've known you, you're the closest to a son if I'd ever had one. I have no one else to pass on my legacy to, and I want that to be you. Those men you saw here tonight don't have what it takes to be a true leader. Yes, they may lead their own men, but sometimes, even leaders need leaders. To keep them in line, to hold them accountable…to set a good example. None of them are good examples. They reek of death, of greed, of filth. But you—*you* have the heart of a lion. You're courageous, fiery and compassionate. I *envy* that. But I know that once I step down, the next generation of Pieces will have a strong, bold and smart example to look up and aspire to be."

"Wait, what are you saying?" Sean asks.

"I've arranged for you to become my successor."

Sean's speechless. Literally speechless.

"If you don't want the job, I understand. It's a very heavy burden to bear, and I would hate to put you in the same position that I put myself in all of those years ago. But times have changed and its not like what it used to be. I'm giving you the choice. And if you choose not to do it, I understand. But I'll leave everything in your care—all of my material possessions including foreign properties, bank accounts and businesses. Everything."

"But what will be left for you?"

Scully places his hand on Sean's shoulder. He sighs.

"From the moment I met you, I knew I'd found the one. The one who'd replace me. The one I could train to carry on mine and the old man's legacy, with enough room to create their own. It's not all drugs, laundering, and politics. There's a true passion for the people. There's true leadership in this role where your influence spreads further than you'd ever thought possible. What you use that influence for is also your responsibility. My responsibility, in a world that I created was to pass it on to someone who wants what's best not only for himself but also for the people he serves.

Our money, albeit comes from drugs and other illegal activities, it helps to fund and build communities, invests in programs and policies that benefit the people. I consider what I've built to be a light in the darkness. It takes years for policies to pass, get funding and actually make it down to the people it was meant for, if at all. I can do it instantly.

Parks, done. Clinics, check. Housing, built. This business is a means to an end. It was always a means to an end. Sometimes you have to take a little, to give a little. My problem with being in this industry for so long, I'd begun to take more than I was giving back. I'd created a culture of takers and lost my path. Once I began to realize it, it was too late. I've tirelessly been trying to rectify my mistakes by trying to do better, live better. I needed to be a better example to my men. But, these men are past their time as well. You can't tame a wild animal, when you're the one who taught it to be wild in the first place. We need new blood, a new era of men and women who care enough but aren't afraid to get their hands dirty from time to time. I knew when I met you, now was the time for me to move on.

"But, why me?"

"I saw myself in you that day. Right here, in *this* gym, punching *my* bag, pouring your heart and soul into every punch, I saw me in you. But this time, as I approached you, I saw myself as the old man who approached me."

Sean turns to see the old man still whittling his piece of wood. Sean hadn't realized until now that the relationship between the manager and Scully was like that of a father and son.

"Jim helped bring me out of my depression all of those years ago, Sean. When I was going through the roughest time of my life, he found me and gave me a purpose. He taught me the value of a dollar, yes, but he taught me so much more. He showed me that the world is not black and white. It's not cut and dry. There're gray areas that you must determine for yourself how you want to approach it. At the time, I wanted to do everything he did, and even though he ordered me not to get involved, I went behind his back and got into something that only he could get me out of.

"After that, he explained that what he did worked for him in a time where everyone played by the same rules. They were old school gangstas who only operated within an old school circle of trust. Everyone outside of this circle was a threat, especially the next generation of men coming to take what they'd worked so hard for. I being much younger than old Jim and his friends, represented a generation that wasn't welcome. I mistook my generous access and affiliation with Jim as my ticket inside the circle. They wanted me dead, but Jim saved my life and it came at a cost. He sacrificed a lot for me, including his rank and membership in the clan. I couldn't understand why he did so much for me, when I was the *worst* kid in these streets. But I'd soon come to realize that living this life, it's a lonely one. He had nothing, no one. I was it. And he gave up so much, because I was being a dumb kid.

"I asked him to train me to do what he did, but better. Let me put my spin on it and take them all down. He was reluctant at first, but once I explained to him my vision for us, to build a new clan, an empire of districts run by Pieces and Players, making enough capital to mold our communities into what we want it to be, getting involved in the upper level of society to see how far our influence could actually reach...Jim was on board. He'd never thought of taking it past a few neighborhoods, maybe even a city. But the world was quickly changing around him and the old school was on its way out.

"I started building by offering my loyalty and protection to the younger neighborhood gangs popping up all over the cities. Jim gave me cash to offer to them as a token of our new partnership and it was like giving milk to a severely dehydrated baby. They sucked it up and once our numbers were up, we organized and brought down the remaining old schoolers and seized their assets, which much of it were Jim's old assets they took from him to save my life.

"But either way, everything has its cycle. Jim is the last remaining OG but he *trained* me to take over. He didn't allow himself to be. Now it's time for me to train *you* to take over, before someone else tries to take it from me."

Sean turns to look at the old man, again. This time his hands are shaking, probably from the memories, but still, he carves away at the dwindling piece of wood. His eyes are distant, gray with cataracts, yet there's empathy there, empathy for Sean.

Sean finally finds his voice.

"How does one even begin to process all of that?"

"I get it, it'll take time, and you'll have that, but for now, I need you to go find my daughter. Scully grabs Sean by the shoulders. "I need you to protect my Ruby."

The eavesdropper behind the door is in as much shock as Sean. He can't believe his ears. All this time he'd been right there with Scully, right alongside him, through everything! He'd worked his butt off to be the most profitable

Piece in the ranks. Now this *kid* comes out of nowhere, sheds a few tears, and *he's* the successor! He's furious, but his patience pays off; an address to where his daughter Ruby may be echoes from behind the door. That ought to make things interesting. Sean will *not* be the next Kingpin; he'd make sure of that.

****

Sean pulls up to Sheila's house 2 hours late. He sits in his car for a moment, gathering his thoughts, remembering what'd just happened.

How can it be, he thinks? *How can Ruby be his daughter? She's the complete opposite of Scully! How crazy is it that the man I've been working for over the past few weeks is the father of a girl I've fallen in ...? And he sent me—me— to find and protect her?*

This is too much. He doesn't know what to do, let alone where to start. How can he protect her? He'd almost gotten her killed when they first met, because he let himself get distracted. How can he protect her from something if he doesn't even know what he's protecting her from? Who's after her, and why?

Endless thoughts play in his mind but he's void of any

helpful solutions. He can't tell her that there are people after her, can he? He can't tell her that he's involved in a network of Kingpins and drug lords, and that he's next in line to take over. What can he tell her? Can he trust Sheila? Tell *her* what's going on, so she can keep Ruby safe? He doesn't know but he can't waste any more time sitting in front of the address Scully gave him.

Sean peers inside the living room window. He watches a happy group of people move around, setting up for a fun evening of food and games. Ruby looks stunning as always. Her brilliant smile forces his, but he feels a knot forming in the pit of his stomach. The daughter of a Kingpin, the most wanted woman in the city is sitting right there, waiting… for him.

Chapter 2

Mike sits at the table in Tony's conference room, staring at the other players with complete disgust. They glare back, silently letting him know that they didn't forget about what happened the last time they'd met.

Chino cracks his knuckles while Terrance silently mouths obscenities from across the table. Mike, not breaking eye contact, surprisingly maintains his cool. He isn't afraid of them. He lights a cigar, takes a long pull and blows smoke into Chino's direction. Chino doesn't move. Neither does he.

"You know the guy who used to be here before you, the one we caught stealin'?" Chino asks.

Mike doesn't acknowledge the question. Chino continues.

"Well that's the story Tony tells people, anyway."

"Tell him what really…what, what really happened…tell him," Terrance stutters, giggling like a crazed hyena.

Hakim and Malcolm exchange glances. Terrance's stuttering problem is annoying beyond belief. They often thought Terrance was prescribed Ritalin as a child but Chino took him under his wing anyway. Terrance, like a kid brother to Chino, follows him around between gigs. He pretty much worships the ground Chino walks on and Chino loves it.

"He didn't steal nothing, he was just mouthy, sort of like you. So, I put my nine in his mouth and shut him up for good."

Terrance slams his fists on the table like a mad man, holding his sides with laugher. Chino cracks a crooked smile and lazily waves his hand, telling Terrance to relax.

Hakim deeply exhales, wondering how in the world this man was able to make a single cent at all. He's a complete idiot.

Mike laughs out loud, first to himself and then, to his aggressive audience. The tip of the cigar wedged in the side of his mouth glows red with each chuckle. The more he laughs, the more Chino's crooked smile morphs into a serious scowl.

"What the hell is so funny?" Chino sneers.

Mike shakes his head. He takes the cigar out of his mouth and taps the ashes into a small crystal ashtray.

"What's so funny is that for someone who hates mouthy people, you sure don't know when to shut up, do you?" He points to Terrance.

"This…runny-nosed…3-year old, elementary-school reject cackles like a witch in heat and I don't see you putting your nine in *his* mouth! You're full of shit Chino. Your threats mean nothing."

Hakim and Malcolm clear their throats. Chino shoots them a look.

"Let me tell you something," begins Chino as Tony walks into the room.

Tony takes his seat at the head of the table as usual and waits for complete silence.

"Can't I leave y'all grown ass men in a room for a few minutes without you trying to kill each other? It's like raising children. Grown *men* and you can't even get along for two minutes without wanting to rip each other's heads off."

Tony massages his temples.

"I called you all here because there is a code red emergency."

The men straighten up.

"The big boss called me and the other Pieces together tonight to discuss something extremely urgent, so I need you fellas to listen carefully."

The men focus on Tony, putting their issues to the side for now.

"Like me, every Piece is giving a speech to their men tonight, but mine is a little different."

Mike and the rest of the Players are glued to Tony, listening intently so as not to miss a single word. They couldn't have guessed in their wildest imaginations what Tony is about to tell them.

"About fifteen years ago, this city was a much different place than it is today. You think there's poor, struggling, hungry people out there now? This is a dream compared to what it used to be. Gang wars plagued the community, and failing crime families fought to the death over what was left. One by one, families that had been established for decades, began to fall at the hands of neighboring territorial gangs.

Young, ambitious and hungry goons formed teams to ransack shipments, assassinate heads of families, flood the market with less potent product, and then reintroduce a higher potency at a higher price under a different street name.

The problem with *these* new people was that as smart as they thought they were, they didn't understand the importance of organization. They needed to cover more ground to make more money, but because of the whole 'crabs in a barrel shit,' these newbies often split from one group to run their own and their friends soon became their competitors.

This sparked a new era of gang wars. The first phase was to get rid of the ancient family dynasties in New York, and once they were wiped out, the new gangs fought each other for the top."

Mike is hungry to hear more of the origins story. He finds himself leaning in like a child at story time.

"There was one man, at the time, who understood the dynamics and logistics of organized crime," Tony continues.

"It's as if he had wisdom beyond his years with a certain flair for creativity, business and resources. At his age, it was impossible to have as much knowledge as he did. His talent went well beyond what others thought of as simply, miraculous. He used his people skills to empower these new groups to organize and run their groups as businesses under him. Everyone would share resources, retain their territories and maintain respect for their competition turned colleagues in the next boroughs.

"One by one, he approached them with promises of opportunities and wealth, and unsurprisingly, they all signed on the dotted line. Within weeks, the boss had re-mapped territories, trained them to manage and run their boroughs and introduced the strategic system of chess within our infrastructure. Naming the leaders, positions, and boroughs based on chess pieces, established a hierarchy, and brought organization to chaos. He alone, not the cops or the politicians, stopped the gang wars fifteen years ago."

Tony's housekeeper taps on the door and he motions for her to come in. She brings in a cart of glasses, sliced lemons, and a carafe of infused fruit water. She pours Tony's glass first and then makes her way around to the others.

The men in the room, as if awakened from a trance, watch her slowly make her rounds. They're eager for her to finish so they can hear the rest of the story, but Terrance is impatient.

"B-b-boss. What is the code r-r-red about, then?"

Chino slowly shakes his head at him, quietly telling him to be patient.

Tony remains quiet as he sips the refreshing fruity water. He smiles at the old woman as she retreats through the heavy doors, but she cowers under his gaze.

"Supper will be ready soon, sir. Should I set a place for six?" she asks.

"No. They'll be leaving shortly. One'll be fine."

The heavy door shuts behind her and the men are once again alone.

"After so much success within a now-peaceful city, the boss became a major target for one particular group, now a district. Although they signed the contract of alliance, they set their sights higher. He'd made all types of valuable connections, not just with the people in the hood but with low rank-and-file police officers, district attorneys, judges, mayors, governors, *and* police commissioners. He even rubbed elbows with celebrities and made friends overseas to import his newly enhanced product into the country. Our boss was revered but he was also feared and envied by anyone who wanted to hold the title 'Kingpin.'

"One night there was a failed attempt on Scully's life and the lives of those closest to him. They killed one of his friends, a woman who answered the door during a family dinner. They tried to kill everyone in the house including his girlfriend, two little girls, and his best friend, but they were unsuccessful. *They* were killed instead and Scully sent his loved ones away, never to see them again. Not even I knew where they were. He thought it was best to be the only one who knew, for fear that someone outside of his circle would find out and attempt to harm them again."

You could hear a pin drop in the room.

"You would think that a man would break if everything he had was taken from him. You'd think he would've given up, but he didn't. Scully grew stronger and even more aggressive. He became colder and dangerous, but his work became his life. Since I was by his side, the more he worked, the more work there was for me, and the more work we had, the more money we got. It wasn't until tonight that we found out that he regretted *everything* that he had worked hard for, everything that he's done to get to where he is…to where *I* am, to where *you* are…today."

26

Mike notices the change in Tony's tone. Tony pounds his fists.

"He wants to be a family man now, to leave all of this behind. He wants to live his life the way he thinks he *should* have lived it all along. Scully has changed."

Tony stands up and walks around the room, forcing everyone's eyes to follow him.

"He wants out, boys. But if he wants out, where does that leave us? Huh? Are all contracts null and void? Does that give the boys in blue permission to come in and tear us down? We've worked *way* too hard...*I've* worked way too hard, and I will *not* be left behind to deal with the fall out because our once fearless leader wants to play daddy all of a sudden!"

"Daddy?" Malcom asks.

"Boss, what do you mean, he wants to play *daddy?*" asks Chino.

"Scully wants out so that he can finally be a father to the little girl he let get away from him fifteen years ago. Or maybe I should say he sent her away and now he wants her back."

"I don't g-g-get it boss. Wha-what little girl?"

"Oh, for cryin' out loud! Haven't you all been listening to me?! One of the little girls in the house was his daughter and he wants to give all of this up so he can be with

27

her, dammit!" Tony yells out of frustration. "I swear, I work with a bunch of idiots!"

Mike lets out a low chuckle, but Chino catches it.

It was all starting to make sense now, they were all beginning to understand, but Chino asks, "So, what's gonna happen now, what are we gonna do?"

"Ok," begins Tony, "This is what Scully *wants* us to do. It just so happens that his daughter is missing..."

"How did she go miss-...," Hakim cuts in.

"It doesn't *matter* how she went missing!" Tony yells, "What matters is that she's missing and *we* know where to find her."

"We do?" asks Malcolm.

"Yeah, we do." Tony smiles.

Mike remains quiet. Something doesn't sound right. The Tony he knew was smart and had dignity! He's a family man, so how could he be so furious at Scully for trying to have a family for himself?

"So," Tony continues, "all the other Pieces have told their Players to do surveillance and if they *happen* to see her to call it in," he rolls his eyes. "What are the chances that they would *happen* to see her? We're to let him know so that he can call her 'parents' to come and pick her up," he says, singing the words like a lullaby.

Terrance gets a big kick out of Tony's singing and begins to do his signature laugh until Chino gives him a big kick underneath the table.

"But we're going to do something different. We're going to find and kill her so that he has no future to look forward to but here's the added bonus."

They lean in closer as he signals them forward with his gold ridden pudgy finger.

"We're going to kill that good for nothing book keeper, Sean, as well."

The men look around at each other again. They just met the guy a few days ago and already Tony wants him dead. They have no idea what Sean has to do with the missing girl, but Tony would soon answer that question.

Mike swallows hard. He thinks about the dinner he'd hosted the other night and how happy his little cousin was when she was with Sean. He saw Ruby's eyes light up when Sean smiled at her. He caught them playfully intertwining their fingers when they thought no one was watching and at the end of the night he witnessed how hard it was for them to say goodbye, lingering until the very last moment.

He hadn't realized until now how happy Sean made her, how much he really cared. He'd always been so overprotective of Ruby. He never stopped to think about her feelings when he came between her and her close male friends she'd introduced him to on his semi-annual trips to his Aunt Marcia's house in Jersey.

Those guys probably did want something more, he thought, but Sean was different. He saved Ruby's life, for God's sake. Mike would be damned if Tony was going to make him or anyone else take Sean away from the person he loved so much.

"For some reason," Tony continues, "Scully trusts this kid Sean so much he's made *him* his successor over me! Can you believe that? Over ME!"

To Mike, Tony seems delirious. He can't finish a thought without his emotions getting the best of him. He's never seen his boss so unraveled before.

"With Sean out of the way, there will be no one left to take over and Scully will have no other choice but to appoint *me* in his place! How great is that, huh? We can literally kill two birds with one stone!" he laughs.

Everyone but Mike appears to have no qualms with going along with this plan. Mike struggles to bite back his protest.

"Now, how we're going to go about this is, after Sean is dead, of course, we'll take the girl somewhere and then tell Scully that we've spotted her. I'll figure out a way to get him down there so when the family comes into town to retrieve her, we can take them *all* out once and for all!" Tony shouts, spinning around to catch everyone's reactions.

Their faces show more concern for the state of Tony's well-being than excitement at his "well" thought-out plan. They may be a group of dangerous men, but they specialize in running a tight ship in the streets to protect their product. They're not guns for hire. They've handled dirty jobs before, ended a few lives, but usually it was to protect their territories. This is different. Tony wants them to kidnap and murder the daughter of the Kingpin! The man who provides for them all. None of them jump to the challenge, but they already know they have no choice.

"I failed once but I won't fail again." Tony takes a seat exhausted from his tirade. "This time they'll all die and *I* will be the Kingpin and you all will be divided among all five boroughs as my Pieces!"

Chino, Terrance, Hakim, and Malcolm's eyes widen in disbelief as they jump out of their chairs, wild with excitement, slapping each other on the back.

"We're gonna be Pieces!"

Mike remains seated and attempts to speak up over the noise.

"So, Tony, I don't get it. *You* were the one who

arranged to assassinate Scully and his family fifteen years ago?"

Tony's smile fades but not completely. The others quiet down and look at Mike as the negative Nancy they already take him to be.

"Yeah...that was me all along and lucky for him he didn't tell me anything about where his family fled because I would've finished the job a long time ago."

"That's crazy, man, he was your boy...he trusted you!" Mike says angrily.

Chino has heard enough.

"Yo man, you got a problem or something? I'm sick and tired of your-

"It's ok," Tony holds up his hand to quiet him. "Mike is a good man, he has morals."

Chino looks at Tony and sits down, straightening his clothes as he almost came out of them.

"I see your point, Mike, but I want you to see mine. I'm a man with pride and it's hard for me to take orders from another man who claims to be superior to me. I've always had to put up a facade like I'm this humble man, when I'm not. I want the world, I want to own it, control it, and rule it, but, the way *I* see it. I can't have the world if someone else already claims it. The only way for me to accomplish my dreams is to take from Scully what I feel is mine." Tony turns to Malcolm and says, "Give it to him."

Malcolm picks up a dark blue duffel bag, removes an oversized black hoodie and hurls it at Mike. Mike eyes Tony questioningly.

"What do you expect for me to do with this?"

"This, Mike, is your black hood. It represents power, it represents strength, and if you wear it well, it'll make you feel like you have the power to control anything. Only *my* people are entrusted to wear it to fulfill the duties and obligations bestowed upon them." Tony focuses his eyes on Mike as if no one else were in the room.

"The other night when Malcolm came to your house and you gave him the home address to the club owner who had reneged on his payments for the fifth time, Malcolm went to his home. He slaughtered his wife, his children, and his mother in front him. Finally, after he prayed and begged for it, Malcolm put a bullet between his eyes. But seeing as how he didn't have a tongue to beg with or hands to pray with, I don't possibly see how that did him any good." Tony laughs.

Mike's eyes widen in fear, in disbelief.

"You see, Malcolm had the strength to accomplish this and with strength he has the power to control his own destiny. And this here," he points to the black hood, "is *your* destiny."

Mike is appalled. His insides twist and his heart almost explodes from the anger welling up inside him. Knowing that Tony had been a part of such a horrific tragedy…the thought sickens him to his core.

"I've had my moment in that hoodie once too," Tony says as he leans back in his chair. He stares into the air as if remembering a fond memory.

"Scully and I always took care of 'business' as we called it. There was always someone who didn't pay their fees, someone who ratted to the police or someone who was trying to take over our territories. But Scully was a man's man. He liked to do *everything* himself. He used to take joy in taking someone's life. Well, not so much joy—joy is the wrong word. It was his duty and he did it well. He didn't like it, but if it had to be done, it had to be done!

"So, one day about 9 years ago," Tony continues, "he tells me I'm worthless 'cause I always sent someone else to do my dirty jobs for me, but what's the point of having men if you can't use them? The point was, Scully refused to have leaders at the top who cowered behind their men. He said I'll never understand what it's like to be a man like *him*. Then he told me not to come back around until I can do the unforgivable and learn live with it.

I was so pissed I took a couple of people from my

'special elite' and put on one of those hoodies. I went to Queens and sat in a train yard, waiting for someone to come by so that I could prove to myself and to Scully, once and for all, that I am a *man*! So, I waited until I saw a man walking by alone holding a stupid teddy bear with a little necklace."

Mike gasps as he looks up from cleaning his fingernails.

"I told him to give it to me and he refused. I didn't really want it but I wanted him to stand there just long enough to look into my eyes, so that he would see that *I* was the one who was going to take his worthless life. *I* was the one who would control his destiny."

Mike clenches his fists tightly, his fingernails form half-moons in the palms of his hands, drawing blood from the pressure.

"After I ran him down, I almost missed my opportunity because people started running towards us from all directions. My guys kept begging me to leave him there and forget about it. But, something told me to take the shot anyway and what do you know, I got him. Scully was right. For the first time in my life I felt like…a real man."

Tony glares at Mike and slowly but sternly says, "Now, put it on, and prove to me that you, Mike, are a man."

Burning tears build behind Mike's eyes as Tony

explains, in great detail, how *he* murdered his uncle, Sheila's father, in cold blood. The knot in his throat tightens. His spirit is as heavy as cement.

All of this time, he'd thought Tony was at least decent, if not good. He gave him a new start, showed him that he could finally trust people. But now, Mike's heart breaks as he remembers how he lied to Sheila earlier that day. He has to tell her, but how?

His train of thought is interrupted as Hakim asks, "So how do we know who we're looking for? Where are we supposed to go?"

Tony smiles again and pulls from his pocket his cell phone with the image of a girl and tosses it into the center of the table.

"You're going to 235 Sutton Ave, Queens."

Mike loses his breath. He quickly slides the phone off of the table and out of Chino's reach. He can't believe what he's seeing. He feels lightheaded.

"The girl's name," Tony says, "is Ruby."

Chapter 3

Sean nervously taps on Sheila's front door with thoughts from his earlier encounter with Scully still haunting him. His thoughts are interrupted by flashbacks of him and Ruby standing on this very same doorstep only weeks earlier. He remembers how terrified she was after he'd protected her the night of her parents wedding. But, in another flashback he recalls how she stared into his eyes on their first date, wanting him, begging him silently to kiss her.

He wanted to. He wanted to do that and more, but he settled for a simple passionate kiss on her head instead. A beautiful, sweet, and smart woman like Ruby deserved to be treated like one. They'd have plenty of time for everything else, or so he hoped.

She felt safe with him. Whenever she's with him, that's exactly how she should feel, he thinks. The way she makes *him* feel, it was as if she'd awakened something inside of him he thought had long died. The spark he saw in her eyes that night was the spark that jolted his heart to beat like never before.

Now, everything is different. One visit with Scully and his whole life has changed. Forget about the new role Scully offered him, he'd think about that later. What about Ruby?

This so-called 'fifteen-year feud' between his boss and this unknown enemy has put her life in extreme danger, more danger than he's ever experienced.

Sean forces away the thoughts of what could possibly happen to Ruby if she were to get captured. His stomach twists and he grabs his abdomen to quell the plummeting sensation just as the front door swings open.

"Sean, finally, you're here!" Sheila says smiling from ear to ear, happy to see him and glad that they can finally eat. As she rushes to embrace him, she notices him holding his stomach and his face seems a little pale.

"Are you ok? What's wrong?"

"Oh, nothing," Sean says, bringing his arms to his sides. "I think my stomach is talking. I can smell the food from out here!"

"Well, that makes the two of us because yah girl Ruby wouldn't let any of us eat until you arrived," she laughs.

"I'm sorry. I shouldn't have kept you waiting for so long. I had to handle something really quick, but it took longer than I expected. I apologize."

"There's nothing to apologize for, handsome. As long as you made it here, you're still good in my book." Sheila gives him a quick peck on the cheek and directs him to the dining room.

Sheila's not sure if Sean is being completely honest with her, but at least he's here and that's what matters. She doesn't think she can take a whole evening of Ruby sulking and letting all of this good food go to waste. *Who am I kidding*, Sheila thinks. *If I have anything to do with it, it won't.*

Ruby enters the dining room from the kitchen. She removes the lids covering the food on Sheila's mahogany dining table with such excitement. She'd heard the doorbell ring and knowing it had to be Sean, flew into action making sure their spread they worked so hard on, was perfect.

Delicious aromas overwhelm the room as Sean walks in. Ruby catches his gaze and gets lost in his eyes, which devour every inch of her. She fights to keep from melting as his lips turn into that magnetic smile she adores. Although he's an hour late, she would've waited for him all night just to see that smile. The rush of excitement flooding through her confirms that the wait was worth every minute.

After narrowly escaping Pam's attempt to kill her in the park the other night, Ruby refuses to continue to let the idea of a past friendship dictate how she should feel now.

Sean was right about Pam all along. She never should've let her come between her and her feelings for him. Now, she can finally open up to him without reservation.

Nothing will stop her now. Sean is all hers.

"So, are y'all just gonna stare at each other all night or nah?" Sheila asks as she walks past Sean and into the dining room. "Is we gonna eat, or are we gonna tear this food up?"

"Shut up, Sheila," Ruby laughs as she tosses a hand towel at her cousin. She turns her attention to Sean. "I'm so glad you made it," she says as she quickly crosses the room to embrace him.

"Are you crazy? I wouldn't have missed this for the world," He opens his arms and hugs her tightly, but Ruby jerks backwards.

"What's wrong, are you ok?"

"Ha...yeah...I just had a little accident," she lies, "I'll tell you about that later."

She wants to tell him what had happened between her and Pam in the park but now is not the time. Now, it's time to eat.

"Okay," Sean sounds pretty perplexed. He's not sure what the "accident" could be, especially considering what he'd recently learned about her and her family's history. He'd been temporarily freed from his troubling thoughts when he first saw Ruby but now they'd returned. Seeing her, here, at the address given to him by her father, made everything all the more real.

Sean waits for Ruby and Sheila to sit down. He proceeds to take his seat as David walks in from the kitchen wiping his wet hands on a paper towel.

"Finally," he laughs, "We can eat." David extends his hand and warmly greets Sean. "Hi, I'm David, a friend of Sheila's. It's nice to meet you. I've heard so much about you."

"Sean, and it's nice to meet you as well," Sean replies. "I can't say that I've heard much about you but it's still a pleasure."

"That's a good thing, I guess," David laughs in Sheila's direction. Sheila flirtatiously cuts her eyes at him in response.

"So enough of the formalities, let's eat!"

At once, they all dig in. Ruby and Sheila really put their culinary skills on display tonight. Fried chicken, maple-baked salmon, an assortment of veggies, loaded baked potatoes, and cornbread. The food was worth the wait as they devour it guilt-free.

Throughout dinner, the couples chat about topics from music to politics to movies. Sheila and David are passionate speakers, especially since they both work in industries that serves their communities. Sheila, the most opinionated of the group, has finally found her match in David. Ruby suspects this is what attracts them to each other in the first place.

Sean, lost in his thoughts, chimes in wherever he can but he can't stop thinking about how both roads between Ruby and Scully have led him to the same exact place tonight.

It's as if I were meant to be here, Sean thinks. *I don't think I could've avoided this if I tried. I don't know the first thing to do. I obviously can't tell Ruby. There's a reason why her real father won't do this himself. What is it?*

His stomach turns in knots every time Ruby smile's. It had gotten worse when she gently kissed and hugged him. His mind races but he's brought back into the moment by the sound of someone calling his name.

"Sean...earth to Sean...are you ok?" Sheila asks.

He looks up to see everyone staring at him.

"Oh yeah...I'm sorry. I was just thinking about something," Sean replies. "What was the question?"

"Forget the question. I wanna know what you were over there thinking about! Care to share?" Sheila inquires.

"Sheila!" Ruby scolds. "Don't mind her, she's being ridiculous. We don't really need to know your business."

"What?!" laughs Sheila. "Yes, we do!"

David shakes his head at her, amused, while digging into the garlic-roasted asparagus for thirds. Sheila notices the amount of sweat pouring out of Sean's forehead and neck but chooses to keep that observation to herself. Something is definitely wrong. It seems to her, the more he senses her looking at him, the wetter his collar gets.

"I'm gonna go to the rest room for a second. Which way?"

"This is a house, Sean. We don't have rest rooms. We have bathrooms and its down the hall and to the left," Sheila lightly jokes while watching him politely excuse himself from the table. The wheels in her head begin to turn.

"You think he's ok in there?" David asks a bit concerned.

"I don't know," says Sheila. "He looked a little off when he came in here but I thought it was just because he was late."

"You think he doesn't want to be here?" asks Ruby, suddenly feeling insecure. "He didn't look like he was paying attention to our conversation. He's barely looked at me since we finished eating."

"Of course, he wants to be here Rube. Why would you say that?" Sheila asks.

"If a man doesn't want to be somewhere, trust me, he won't go," says David reassuringly.

"So, what does that say about *you,* mister?" Sheila flirts, leaning closer to him.

"Obviously it says that I wanted to come too," David

leans in and kisses her on her nose. Ruby rolls her eyes, wishing the awkwardness between her and Sean would let up so that they could enjoy each other's company like Sheila and David. She wonders if he could be having second thoughts.

Sheila's phone vibrates with a text message.

SHEILA, IT'S MIKE. YOU HAVE TO LEAVE YOUR HOUSE NOW! NO TIME TO EXPLAIN.

Sheila stands, pushing her chair backwards.

"What is it, what's wrong?" asks David. He wipes his mouth with his napkin and tosses it onto the table.

"I-, I don't know... I just got a text from my cousin Mike but I don't understand."

"Well call him back, Shells," demands Ruby.

"I'm trying to but he won't answer." Sheila paces around the room desperately trying to call him back, but each time she receives no answer. "Wait, he just sent another one."

I CAN'T ANSWER THE PHONE RIGHT NOW BUT YOU HAVE TO GET OUT NOW, SHELLS, NOW!

She texts him back. *WHAT IS THIS ABOUT, MIKE? WHAT'S GOING ON?*

Mike texts her back almost immediately. *WHO'S THERE WITH YOU? ALL OF YOU NEED TO LEAVE. DON'T GRAB ANYTHING, JUST GO!*

Sheila frantically texts Mike while ignoring Ruby's

questions and requests to read the text messages aloud. David stands by watching her, not sure as to why Sheila is ignoring them. Sheila continues to text. *IT'S ME, RUBY, MY FRIEND DAVID & SEAN. Y? WTH IS GOING ON?!*

Sheila waits and continues to wait for a response. Her chest heaves as she clenches her cell phone. Ruby continues to nag her with questions.

Sean, completely oblivious, walks in on a scene completely different from when he'd left.

"Is everything ok?" he asks Ruby.

"I don't know what's going on," she replies, frustrated. Finally, the last message from Mike comes in.

U WERE RIGHT ABOUT THE BLACK HOODIES & NOW THEY'RE ON THEIR WAY 2 UR HOUSE. THEY'RE COMING 4 RUBY AND SEAN! GET OUT OF THERE NOW. WE'RE ALMOST THERE!

****

Sean, Ruby, and Sheila follow David into his house without a single word exchanged. They all take a seat in his living room, unable to make any sense out of what had just happened.

The whole 30-minute car ride had been even more uncomfortable as Ruby kept asking Sheila to explain what Mike's messages said and why they were leaving. Sheila continued to ignore her, snapping at her a few times telling her to drop it so that she could think, which sent Ruby into a fit. She doesn't understand why Sheila's holding back from her. They had gotten even closer in the past few weeks, so why is she acting so strange all of a sudden?

David's hospitality is appreciated as he goes out of his way to make them all comfortable. He doesn't know the content of the text's but he knows that keeping them all safe is his top priority right now. He disappears into the kitchen to fetch beverages and to prepare for a very long night ahead.

"Sheila, I'm going to ask you again and this time I want an ANSWER!" Ruby's face is red with anger and she has no intentions of backing down.

Sheila glares at her hot-headed cousin.

"Why in the world are we over here at David's house?" Ruby asks. "What is going on?"

"I don't know, Ruby, all I know is, I got a text from Mike telling us to leave the house and to be quick about it. I don't *know* what else is going on." Sheila says dramatically.

"You're lying!" Ruby screams. "You know way more than you're telling me. Because if it was that freaking simple you would have said that earlier instead of ignoring me the whole way here!"

Sheila is holding back for the sake of not arguing, but Ruby is pushing her luck.

"Ruby, you need to sit down and relax," Sheila warns through gritted teeth.

"Why? Why should *I* have to sit down and relax? Everyone else around here is so relaxed. It's like no one even cares about what's happening here." Ruby begins to pace the living room.

"I mean, is someone after us?" she scoffs, "and, and if they are, why? Why did Mike text you to tell you that? How does he know, what is he involved in? Why are we here?"

"RUBY, I DON'T KNOW! ALL RIGHT?" Sheila yells. "I am just as confused as you are so sit the fuck *down* 'cause *you* are aggravating me!"

Ruby's mouth is wide open. She can't believe it. She never expected Sheila to speak to her like this. Sean sits there with his elbows on his knees and his head in his hands. His head is pounding from the throbbing migraine that'd crept in.

'Could this, be it? Could this be what Scully warned me about? Sean wonders. *How is Mike involved? What did the messages say?* The more he tries to come up with answers, the more painful the migraine becomes.

David doesn't want to get involved but he knows the last thing they all need is for the girls not to get along. They'll never solve anything that way.

"You know what, Shells, I thought we were closer than this. I just found out that *my* parents have been hiding secrets from me for years, making me believe in some stupid fairytale, when my life, it turns out, is a freaking nightmare." Ruby takes out the case file she'd brought with her and throws it on the floor, its gruesome pictures and documents falling out of the sleeve.

"Pam, whose past is linked to mine, tried to kill me yesterday. *Kill* me, Sheila! Now, we had to leave *your* house in a panic in the middle of the night and no one can tell me *anything*?" Ruby moves closer to Sheila as she fights back tears.

"And you...you and I are supposed to be in this together. I thought I could trust *you* if not anyone else, but I see you're just like them." Tears streak her face. "Who can I trust now?"

Sheila stands in silence, ashamed because she knows Ruby is right. But she stands her ground. It's for her own good, whether she knows it or not.

Still not getting the answers she wants, Ruby retreats into one of the rooms David has set up.

"Ruby," Sean calls after her. She slams the door behind her. Not even Sean can comfort her now.

He sits down feeling useless. This night started out badly at the gym and when he arrived at Sheila's it quickly went from bad to worse. Inside he holds onto a horrible secret, sworn to keep it as if his life depended on it. But with *everyone's* lives in danger now, he wonders what he should do. *Can I trust David, to tell him the truth? This guy is a cop! If he works for Scully, it would get back to him that I snitched and I'd be killed for sure.* Sean is overwhelmed. *But Ruby's life is at stake and Scully told me the most important job I have to do is to protect her. How can I do that when I don't even know what's going on?*

Sean continues to wallow in his thoughts while he watches David console Sheila, who is breaking down by the minute. It seems there's nothing David can say to make her feel better.

"She's right, you know. And you were right. I should have just told her. I should have just told her." she cries.

"Listen Sheila, everything will be ok. She just needs a moment to gather herself." David passes her a box of tissues. "You've both been through so much these past few weeks and you've kept most of your feelings bottled up. Just take a moment to get yourself together. If you need to cry, cry, but don't beat yourself up. She's probably up there doing the same thing. I'll talk to her in a minute but baby, you need to breathe."

Sheila takes in a few staggered breaths, trying to compose herself but she can't stop herself from crying. Sean feels a knot forming in his throat. He hates to watch them in pain because of something that had nothing to do with them. They just happened to be caught up in the crossfire of a fifteen-year-old feud. But something isn't making sense. He's just now realizing that Sheila, David, and Ruby know a little more than he or Scully for that matter.

"Um, Sheila…," Sean repeats her name to get her attention.

She forgot that Sean was in the room.

"I don't mean to intrude or anything but what's going on? Did I hear Ruby say Pam tried to *kill* her?" he asks. He's even more confused now. Could Pam be in on it too? How could she? She and Ruby were kids back then. Nothing is making sense.

Sheila looks at him and wipes her eyes. She's beginning to calm down but, still a little frustrated.

"Yeah, apparently, your girl followed you that night when we went to Mike's for dinner and saw you and Ruby together in the street. She lured Ruby to the park, questioning her about it and *then* stabbed her in the side with a kitchen knife."

"What? How? I-, I haven't spoken to her in a couple of weeks! How did she...why did she?" Sean can't even finish his thought. There's no way that he could protect Ruby from anything if he didn't even notice his psychotic ex-girlfriend following him all the way to the Bronx. *What's* wrong *with her? What's wrong with him?*

He'd never been this way before in his life! He was always on his A game, always watching his back in these streets until...Ruby. A lightbulb goes off. *She's* the distraction. When his mind is on her, it's on nothing else and each time it's placed her in danger.

Sean realizes something. *I can't do this. This job Scully needs for me to do, I can't do it. I have to tell Sheila and David what I know. They're the only ones who can probably stay focused enough to keep Ruby safe.*

"...because she's a psycho bitch, that's why," Sheila finishes his sentence. "She's still in love with you and if she can't have you, no one can."

Sean is stunned. He knew Pam was crazy but this...

"What was she questioning Ruby about," Sean asks. "Was it about me? How did she get Ruby up there in the first place?"

51

"Sheila, I don't know if it's such a…"

"It's ok, David, he should know. As a matter of fact, I wouldn't be surprised if Sean doesn't know more than he's leading us to believe," she says. She stares at Sean, not moving a muscle. David looks back and forth between the two of them. He is just as lost as Sean.

"What? What are you talking about?" Sean asks.

"I think you know exactly what I'm talking about. Don't play stupid with me."

Could she know his secret and his purpose for being there besides dinner?

"I-, I don't know…"

"Sheila, obviously, the guy doesn't know what you're talking about so just spit it out!" says David.

Sheila rolls her eyes at him. "You know, for a cop you suck at interrogating. Anyone with eyes can *clearly* see that he's tripping up on his words because he knows something."

"Sheila, even *I* don't know what you're talking about, just say it!" David pleads. He understands Ruby's frustration a whole lot more now.

She shakes her head and turns her attention back to Sean whose face is turning paler by the second.

"Fine. The reason why we left my house in such a hurry is because my cousin Mike just happens to be involved with a group of guys in *black hoodies...* " emphasizing this last part for David, who had doubted her connection between the deaths in the case file and the black hoodies since the beginning of their investigation. "...who were making their way over to *my* house at that exact moment."

Sean is confused, "What? Why?"

"Yeah, why were they coming to your house, Sheila?" David asks.

Sheila keeps her face glued to Sean's to catch any sign of a reaction.

"Because they are after Ruby *and*...Sean."

Sean springs to his feet and starts pacing around the room. It's getting way too hot. He takes his sweater off.

Sheila watches him pace as David rains questions down on her one after another. She doesn't answer. She keeps her eyes on Sean. As he returns to the middle of the room, he stops to pick up one of the pictures that had fallen out of Ruby's case file sleeve. He studies it closer and loses his breath. Dizziness overcomes him as he connects the image to the story Scully had shared with him earlier. *What have I gotten myself into?* He thinks. *All I wanted was an opportunity to start a new life and now I'm mixed up in all of this shit. A world of death—a world Scully wants me to run.* Everything he'd ever felt for his boss melts into pure disgust. He'd admired him and was inspired by his story, but this? *Whatever Scully wants to do, he can do it without me. I won't follow in his footsteps.* But there is still one outstanding issue: Ruby.

"What is it about that picture, Sean?" Sheila asks, raising her voice over David's questions. She's completely tuned him out and is now laser focused on Sean—she notices which photo he'd picked up.

"I know this man," Sean replies, almost mechanically. Beads of sweat form on his face. It's as if he's in a trance-like state and Sheila is his hypnotist.

David quiets down.

"*How* do you know this man, Sean?" she asks slowly, quietly.

"I, I work for him..."

"And...?"

"And I already knew Mike before meeting y'all at his house," he admits.

"Why are they after you?" She asks. Sheila continues to interrogate him and this time David watches silently. Sean stares at the wall ahead of him as if he were looking through it.

"Someone must have found out that he wants me to succeed him," he whispers as he connects the dots aloud.

"Sean...*Sean*..."

He continues to stare blankly into the wall. It was as if everything from the past few weeks had come rushing back to him at that moment like a movie reel and he couldn't stop it no matter how hard he tried.

'If I had never have gone to that wedding and met Ruby, I wouldn't be here right now," he says. "But this started way before Ruby. It started with Pam. If I hadn't been so stressed over Pam, I probably wouldn't have been in the gym and met Scully. If I hadn't been with her, I wouldn't have been in a financial rut to begin with and wouldn't have needed Scully's money in the first place. If I hadn't been with Pam, I would never have met Ruby." Sean's mind continues to race.

Ruby. This girl is surrounded by chaos and dysfunction and she still has no clue that her life is in danger. She needs protection. She's too precious to everyone in her life, to Scully, to her parents, to her cousins, to me. She's like a precious gemstone and as hard as it is to admit it, I think I...

"Sean..." Sheila's voice pierces through his thoughts very subtly at first but then more harshly.

"*Sean.*"

"Yeah, I'm sorry," he says, shaking his head and rubbing his eyes with both hands.

"How did they know that you were at my house?"

"They must have overheard the boss telling me where

I could find Ruby."

Sheila almost gasps aloud but manages to hold it in. She'd been holding back tears during the entire conversation. She tries to remain calm but at the mention of Ruby's name coming from this guy Sean calls the boss, she almost loses it.

"Your *boss* sent you to my house?"

"Yeah."

"Why?"

"To protect her." Sean's anxiety is increasing again.

Sheila takes in a deep breath. She can feel him slipping away from her. She's about to lose him but she has to know. Her throat tightens but she pushes herself to ask a question that she's not sure she wants to hear the answer to.

"To protect her from what?"

Sean takes a deep breath too. He exhales, slowly.

"From those who would want to use her to hurt him."

"And why would he care, what significance does Ruby hold in all of this?" Sheila's tears can no longer be restrained, her face glistens with a mixture of tears and mascara.

Sean faces her. His face is overcome with fear.

"Because, Sheila…he's her father."

Chapter 4

Mike and his crew of miscreants pull up to Sheila's house and park across the street. They sit there for a half hour quietly waiting for a sign of life from within. It's twelve thirty in the morning, a couple of cars are parked in the driveway but it isn't clear if anyone is home or if they are out and coming back soon.

Mike texts nervously trying to find out if Sheila had listened to him after all. He doesn't see her car but Ruby's is still parked in the driveway. He hopes they'd all gotten into Sheila's car and left but he needs to make sure.

"Yo man, you've been texting all night. Why don't you give it a rest? Your screen is lighting up your face!" says Hakim.

"Look, when it comes down to it, I need to handle my business. Just because we're out here in hoodies don't mean the show gotta stop. I got a shipment coming through and I need to handle mine. So, chill out," Mike snaps back.

"Whatever man, just make sure to keep that light down." Hakim continues looking out the window.

Just as quickly as Mike is texting, he's also erasing all outgoing and incoming messages. Sheila finally answers.

YES MIKE, WE'RE OUT OF THERE ALREADY STAYING WITH A

FRIEND. WE NEED 2 TALK. S IS HERE WITH US 2.

Mike responds: *WE JUST GOT HERE. I THINK THEY'RE THINKING ABOUT GOING INSIDE. U CAN'T EVER COME BACK 2 THIS HOUSE UNTIL WE FIGURE SOMETHING OUT. HOUSE MAY BE TRASHED BUT AT LEAST UR SAFE. DO YOU HAVE SOMEWHERE 2 STAY?*

Sheila replies: *MY FRIEND SAID WE COULD STAY HERE WITH HIM. WE NEED TO MEET SOMEWHERE TOMORROW. I'LL LEAVE R HERE CAUSE THE STREETS AREN'T SAFE. TEXT ME IN THE MORNING.*

Mike erases and replies. *OK. I'LL HIT YOU UP LATER. I LUV U.*

Sheila texts back. *I luv u 2.*

"Yo Chino, I think we should just go in, man. Enough of this waitin' around!" says Malcolm.

"If we go inside, we need a game plan. We can't go in there blasting. People are gonna hear it," Chino replies.

"Why would we go in there blasting if we're supposed to take them back alive?" asks Mike. Chino turns around and scowls.

"'Cause, we only need Sean and that Ruby bitch. If anyone else is in there, they get it!"

Mike's blood boils. He's talking about killing his family! He wants to kill him himself right then and there. But a gun fight inside a car isn't smart, especially if he wants to get out of it alive.

"Then why don't we do this? Why don't just two of us go out there and look inside the side and the back windows. If the coast is clear and they aren't home then we don't need to go in and risk blowin' our spot," Mike suggests.

"Negro, what the hell are you on? Opportunities to use my Glock don't come too often. We're still going in whether they're there or not. We gonna wait around 'til they come back if we have to!" Chino says.

"We can't wait around if they don't come back 'til morning," yells Mike. "The whole damn neighborhood will be up by then, our car will be out here and they'll call the cops because they don't recognize it. People do that!"

Hakim and Malcolm, now conscious that someone might be watching *them,* shift uncomfortably in their seats. The houses are too close together for all of them to get out without bringing attention.

"He's got a point," says Malcolm, "We don't want no cops called on us."

"Yo, we OWN the cops!"

"NO, WE DON'T," Mike yells again from the back seat. "Scully owns the cops and if they're called, Scully will find out that we're at the house! No one but Sean is supposed to have that information and he's gonna know Tony is behind it. I know you don't want that, cause if his money stops, all of ours does too. So, tell me again that you want to go into a house and shoot it up for NO reason if no one is in there!"

The car is silent. The tension between Mike and Chino is thick enough to cut. Before Mike came along Chino called the shots, but now it seemed that Mike was smarter and more strategic than them all.

"I call the shots around here." Chino says, trying to maintain his authority. "Malcolm, Hakim, go and peep out the house and see if they in there, if they not, then come right back and we out."

"Nah," says Mike, "Me and your remedial-ass pet Terrance will go. You need two good sets of eyes out here with you. It doesn't take an idiot to look through a window...but I'm pretty sure he'll enjoy the fresh air."

Terrance giggles along with Malcolm and Hakim, seemingly unaware that the joke is on him. Chino throws up his middle finger after Mike as they get out of the car and cross the street.

After walking around the house for a few minutes, Mike glances down at his watch.

"Alright man, let's go. Ain't no one here," Mike says to Terrance.

Terrance jumps down off of a nearby porch chair.

"Don't move or I swear I'll shoot you right where you stand!"

Mike stops. He doesn't move a muscle. Terrance's gun is pointed directly in front of Mike's face as he moves in closer, speaking clearer than Mike has ever heard him speak before. Terrance flips the safety off.

"You filthy bastard, who the hell do you think you are?" says Terrance.

"What are you talking about? Filthy bastard? How old are you, Fifty?"

Terrance grabs him by his collar and spins him around so that his hands are up against the side of the house. Terrance searches him with his gun pointed deep into the middle of Mike's back. He finds Mike's gun, wallet, and cell phone and throws everything to the ground, all but Mike's cell.

"What do we have here?" Terrance starts scrolling through the messages. "You were on this thing all night. I saw your face when the picture of that girl hit the table and now here we are and there's no one home?"

"Who are you? What are you doing?" Mike tries to watch Terrance behind him, yet also trying not to get shot.

"Aw, this is sweet. I love you too. Who was that from, your girl?"

"Uh…yeah…"

"So how come there ain't no outgoing messages saying that you love her for her to say that she loves you too."

"'Cause, man…" says Mike.

Terrance is forcing his gun so hard into his back, Mike winces in pain.

"'Cause what? 'Cause you keep erasing your messages! You think I'm stupid right, everyone thinks I'm dumb? I'm such a dumb idiot, right?!" Terrance yells. "Well guess what? I'm not as stupid as you think. Now tell me why you erased all your messages. It must be something important 'cause you've been doing this all night."

"I erased it 'cause that's my side chick and when I get home, my girl be goin' through my phone. That's why! You know how it is, now get that gun out of my got damn back and tell me what the hell this is about!"

Terrance releases him and tosses his phone back.

"If you're gonna erase messages so that the Mrs. don't see… don't forget to erase the most important one."

Mike glances down at his phone to see the last message he received from Sheila. His heart sinks at the thought that if she didn't heed his warning, she may have ended up dead all because he didn't come clean to her when he had the chance to. She was right, he was a loser and his decisions not only affect him but, they also affect the people he loves.

"Terrance, what is all of this *about,* man?"

Terrance pulls him deeper into the shadows behind the house to be sure they are out of sight and speaks quietly.

"I work for Internal Affairs and I've been planted here to monitor Tony. I play dumb to keep myself off the radar as much as possible. I'm just here to observe and take action if necessary."

Mike, not sure what to make out of it, sizes him up` as if seeing him for the first time.

"I notice lots of things and I notice that you're a bit 'different' from the others. You seem smarter and you're more compassionate than those losers back there. I've never had a chance to be alone with you one on one so I appreciate what you did back there by allowing me to come with you. You made a very smart decision because if anything had gone down, I couldn't have allowed that to happen and I would have blown my cover. There's no way I could've gotten away from them to call for backup but you diffused it quite nicely. And now I can talk to you for a few minutes."

Here is dumb ol' Terrance who isn't actually dumb at all. He's a freaking cop! He still doesn't trust him, though. Mike doesn't like the guys he works with, yes, but cops, he hates them even more. But what choice does he have now that his family is in danger? Can he trust him to help?

"So why are you here?" Mike asks.

"I'm here because there is corruption within the department so deeply rooted, we've had to go undercover on our own to investigate. We've tracked money laundering, drug trafficking, and so forth and so on to this specific drug ring. The police commissioner, Victor Peters, is in a lot of trouble and if I can prove that he gets bribes and payoffs from the Kingpin, Scully, then we can put him away for good. I need to get that red book from Sean. I believe there is enough evidence in there to put them all away for good."

"Why are you telling *me*? How do you know that I won't just snitch on you and let Tony take care of you?" Mike asks.

"Because anyone who has a good heart can see the good in someone else. Your face may be like stone sometimes but I could tell when you found out that poor man and his family were killed, due to something *you* were a part of, you were in pain. You hurt inside and I saw that. I do believe that you have some connection to this girl we're looking for because of how you reacted to the photo."

"If you noticed that, how do I know that no one else did?"

"Don't worry. Those guys are stupid idiots, for real for real. They didn't notice anything. Tony didn't notice either because he was so caught up in his 'woe is me' dramatics. I knew because I've been around him long enough to tell. Besides, I saw a picture of you and some other girl on a nightstand through that window over there."

Mike's eyes widen. He'd forgotten all about the pictures in the house.

"Good thing it was me who came with you and no one else." Terrance picks up Mike's wallet and gun and hands it back to him. He walks back towards the street with Mike in tow.

"Point is," he adds right before they reach the well-lit part of the driveway, "if you do know her, continue to do what you're doing to keep her out of reach. She'll be safer that way."

Mike looks at him with a straight face.

"I don't know what you're talking about."

Terrance smiles and winks at him.

"Exactly my point." He works up a good drool and scampers back to the car. When they get in, Chino is furious.

"Was there anyone in there? I mean damn man, y'all took forever!"

"N- no, no, Chino," Terrance stutters.

"I thought I saw someone but it wasn't who I thought it was," Mike tells him.

Terrance glances back at him from the front passenger seat, understanding what Mike is saying and taking it as a sign of cooperation.

"Well, who was it?" Chino asks, peeling off into the night. Everyone looks at Mike, who wears a satisfied smirk on his face.

"Your Momma."

Chapter 5

While David is upstairs checking in on Ruby, Sheila and Sean sit in the living room, contributing their own pieces to the mystery puzzle to see the larger picture for what it is.

Sean's mind is getting clearer. He feels the weight lifting as he comes clean about what he knows, how he'd met Scully, and why he's associated with him in the first place. Sheila also let him know about the case they are trying to solve and how Ruby's and Pam's lives are affected by it all. Sheila is trusting him with this sensitive information. Hopefully, he won't make her regret it.

The only info Sean could give about Ruby's parents is that Scully is currently in contact with them and will call them to tell them where Ruby is once she's found. Word on the street is, Ruby is Scully's long-lost daughter and she's gone missing.

Because her parents haven't heard from her for days, they feared the worst. They initiated a meeting with Scully, who took it upon himself to conduct a citywide search for his beloved daughter. The only thing is, Ruby's parents and Scully have no idea what they've done. They'd awakened a slumbering dragon and this time, the enemy is stronger than ever.

Sheila shakes her head.

"I told her to call them. She promised me she would call!" She takes a breath. "So, let me get this straight, Sean. You mean to tell me that because Ruby didn't call her parents, like I told her to, of course, they contacted her *father,* who is *your* boss. Correct?"

Sean nods his head.

"Because they thought he could keep an eye out for her and protect her from those who may want to harm *him*?"

"Yes."

"But instead of protecting her, they put her in harm's way by alerting everyone as to who she is, where she may be, and what she means to him?"

"Yes and no," Sean says. He keeps his voice down and slides closer to the edge of his seat.

"Yes, they put her in harm's way by telling everyone who she is, but Scully only told *me* where I could find her. The only other person in that room was the old man but I doubt he had anything to do with it. I don't know who else could've heard us. I didn't say anything to anyone. I would never do that." He thinks about it for a second longer.

"Maybe it was Tony, Mike's boss. You said Mike was on his way over to your house, right? He had to have gotten instructions from him. That's the only way!"

"Okay, don't worry about that. When we speak to Mike in the morning he'll be able to tell us more about it." Sheila stands up and stretches. It's two o'clock in the morning and her eyes are heavy and swollen. Every ounce of energy has drained from her and she needs some rest. They all had a long, long day and she has to be good and prepared for what tomorrow will bring.

"Why don't you call your aunt and uncle and put this whole thing to rest right now? We can be free of all of this and Ruby will be safe, finally," Mike asks.

"For multiple reasons. For one, Ruby would never forgive me for doing that. She has her mind set on solving this secret her parent's have held from her all of her life. I normally wouldn't care and would be the first one on the phone. But, there are other factors here that also have me curious. Those hoodies my cousin mentioned fits a description of a gang that killed my dad when I was a teenager. It's the very reason I'm studying to be a lawyer. The very reason why I work so closely with law enforcement. I never accepted his death as a one off. So, when I saw one of them come to my Mike's house that night, a house he couldn't have afforded only a couple of months ago, I got suspicious.

I want you, Ruby, all of us safe and for this all to be over too, but something inside of me wants to keep pushing, to keep going. And as dramatic as Ruby is, I understand that insatiable itch. The desire is greater than the surrender. That's the best way I can put it."

David descends the stairs carrying blankets, pillows, and a long t-shirt for Sheila to sleep in.

"Hey Sean, Ruby's barely asleep but I told her that you're still here and would stay the night. She'll want to speak to you in the morning. I didn't tell her anything about what you told us, I'll leave you to fill her in on that."

David hands Sheila the t-shirt and tosses the blankets on the couch.

"Sheila, I told her that you were just trying to protect her and that you love her very much. She's still pretty upset but I've calmed her down for now. She understands why you may have held back from her but I reassured her that you will never do it again. She seems to be satisfied with that."

Sheila gives him a peck on the cheek.

"Thanks David, I appreciate that. I'll probably go in there and sleep with her tonight so that I can be close to her," she says as she begins to pick up the linens he'd just dropped onto the couch.

"Uh, I think you should just give her some space and let her sleep it off until the morning. She'll be more refreshed. Besides I thought maybe you'd want to spend a little time together. Take a load off."

Sheila catches his hint while Sean quickly turns his attention elsewhere.

"Then who are these for?"

"Those are for Sean. He's gonna sleep on the couch."

"Sean, is that okay with you, to sleep here I mean." Sheila asks.

"Well I guess I can't go home, can I?" He sounds disappointed.

"No, you can't," David confirms.

"That's cool with me. I'll be out here keeping watch," Sean laughs nervously.

"Well, if you hear anything, holla at me," says David. As he and Sheila make their way upstairs, David turns back to Sean and nods his head towards Ruby's doorway.

****

Sean slowly approaches Ruby's door but, hesitates for a moment before knocking. He doesn't know what to say to her and he isn't even sure if she wants him there to begin with. He's well aware that his suspicious behavior during dinner probably made her feel awkward.

He couldn't take her looking at him the way she did. Her eyes, so full of laughter and love. They drew him in from across the table, making his blood rush and his stomach flip. Her lips invited him to taste more than what was laid out for dinner.

He wanted to lay *her* out and nibble at every part of her. She was so beautiful and her voice was irresistibly sweet, yet laced with sarcastic humor. Her laugh was intoxicating and her smile mesmerized him.

Every time she took a bite of her food, he watched her chew in slow motion, licking her lips just before taking another bite. What he wouldn't give to finally taste them.

The task that Scully had given him was impossible. Thinking about his meeting earlier, his stomach wouldn't allow him to keep his dinner down. He had to take off to the bathroom. Now, everything had turned into a complete investigation on who was after them and why.

Why me, Sean wonders. *If Tony is behind this, why does he want me dead?*

Sean lightly taps on Ruby's bedroom door, hoping not to disturb Sheila and David down the hall. There's no answer. He opens the door slightly to peek inside, hoping his intrusion doesn't alarm her.

She rests on her stomach in the center of the bed with

her head turned opposite from him. Her long, wavy hair is spread wildly on the pillow beneath her and her left hand lays lifeless against the top of her scalp. Unsure if she'd heard him knock, he proceeds to enter without invitation.

The lamp on the side table closest to Ruby illuminates her silhouette, accentuating her slender curves beneath the thin white sheet draped across her body. He gently closes the door behind him in case she's asleep. If he can just sit in a corner and keep watch over her while she rests, he'll feel a lot better. He has to make sure she's safe; after all, he's made a promise to her father to make sure of it.

Knowing more about Ruby's complicated past doesn't make things any easier for him. In fact, he questions whether he's the right man for the job; whether he can truly do what needs to be done to keep her safe.

"Ruby, are you awake?"

"Umm hmmm." She answers sleepily.

Sean sits down on the edge of her bed and faces her.

"I just wanted to come in and check on you. Are you okay?"

"I'm okay now," she sighs. "I'm just so tired of all of this. It's like...I don't know what to think, who to trust or what to do anymore."

Heartbroken, Sean places his hand gently on her leg to

help console her.

"Ruby, you have to understand that the people in your life love you so much that at times, it's hard for them to explain why they do the things they do. They just want to protect you," he reassures her.

Ruby twists around to study him.

"So, I guess they told you everything?"

"They told me enough."

"So, what do you think about it? What do you think about all of this?" She sits up in bed. Her eyes plead for another perspective other than her own, her cousin's or David's.

"I...I don't know what to think honestly. I know that your parents love you very much and whatever it is that happened, they did it for your own good. If they didn't love you then..."

"They wouldn't have tried to hide my past from me?" she guesses.

"Exactly."

"What about you, Sean?" Ruby stares into his eyes. The room is too dark; she can barely see his face but the light from the lamp reflects in them, making them sparkle.

"What *about* me?" he asks quietly. Does she suspect that he's hiding something from her as well? How can she know anything about...?

"Do *you* love me?"

Silence settles between them. Everything between them is so complicated. It's only been a few weeks, but that shouldn't matter.

What if I say it and she holds me to it? What if I can't protect her and then she blames me? I'd become like everyone that's ever told her they love her and let her down.

"Ruby...I-, I care about you...a lot," he begins.

She turns away from him and lies back down.

"I knew you were gonna say that." Disappointment laces her words. She didn't even want to ask him in the first place, it just kind of slipped out. And now she forced his back against a wall and made him tell her his truth. What is wrong with her? How *could* he love her so quickly? He barely even knows her, she thinks. But she knows what she feels in her heart and if it's possible for her to love him, then it's possible for him to love her too.

"Ruby, it's not like that."

"Sean, it's okay. I'd rather you tell me the truth than for you to search for an answer to make me feel better."

"Ruby, look at me," he demands. Sean moves closer to her, just as close as they were on the night of the wedding when he dropped her off at Sheila's house for the first time.

"You didn't let me finish." With a gentle grab of her chin, he softly brushes his lips across hers.

Ruby, helpless within his grasp, breathes deep and long.

"I care about you a lot," he says caressing the back of her neck. He then carefully takes a handful of her hair within his grasp and slowly begins to massage her scalp.

"…and I would never let anything happen to you…" Sean gently tugs on her hair and guides her head backward, slowly, exposing her long slender neck to his hungry eyes. With every other word, he kisses Ruby from her shoulders to her collarbone and upwards until he reaches her mouth again.

"I'd die before I let anything happen to you…"

She moans as his lips graze past the sensitive area on her throat, right beneath her jaw line. He releases her hair, grips her by the waist and pulls her into him. "I knew from the day I met you, you were the one for me." He kisses her, slowly, fully tasting the lusciousness and thickness of her lips, finally.

"From that moment on, all I could think about is you." He kisses her again, this time allowing his lips to linger, longer.

"There is no one else in this world I'd rather be with than you, Ruby." The third time, his mouth finds her soft, warm, wet tongue and he neglects all restraint as he massages it sensually with his.

"You asked me if I love you…"

The dance of their mouths stimulates him in a way that distracts his every thought. Each time she squirms beneath his touch, it drives him mad. All of the blood in his body races through his veins like lightening to his nether regions.

She gasps.

"And the answer is…yes." This time he doesn't stop. With every touch of her lips he falls in love deeper and deeper.

Ruby allows him to explore her, inch by inch, shivering as he trails his strong, thick fingers across every part of her exposed skin. He supports the base of her back with those strong hands beneath her shirt, sending a bolt of electricity throughout each vertebra.

Ruby takes a moment to absorb the magic forming between them and stores it in her memory.

The way Sean licks his lips before he bites the lower half of her mouth drives her close to insane. Ruby, desperate for more, rubs his chest, feeling his mildly hairy, stiff pectoral muscles flexing beneath her fingertips. She hurriedly unbuttons his shirt with her free hand while the other fidgets with his belt buckle.

She hadn't the nerve to touch him before. She'd put so much energy into pretending that she was hardly interested, but now, everything has changed. Everything is different.

Ruby doesn't want to stop. She can't stop. Touching him makes it real. Everything that she'd ever wanted from him, is happening, in this moment. Every thought and fantasy she'd pushed out of her head in the previous weeks comes flooding back and competes to be the first to come to fruition.

Her conscience encourages her to keep going like a cheer squad in the back of her mind. Every reservation she's felt since she'd met him melts away in the heat of passion.

As she pulls off his undershirt, she stops. Her eyes scan over every chiseled muscle and every deep cut in his physique. Sean's chest and abs are tight, his shoulders are wide and sturdy, and his arms—those beautiful, big, strong arms—cocoon her in an embrace she hopes never to be released from.

He is the most perfect man I have ever seen, she thinks. How he got a body like this is unbeknownst to her, but, one thing she does know is, she has never been more in love with anyone than she is with him, right now.

Sean slowly lifts the oversized t-shirt over Ruby's head and drops it onto the floor. She sits there, glowing in the soft golden light from the lamp, wearing a lace thong and nothing else. She doesn't even try to cover her exposed breasts. What's the point? They've come this far. There's no turning back now.

The seductive look in her eyes invites him in, gives him permission to do whatever it is that his heart desires. Whatever it is, she allows herself to willingly submit, something she's never done before, with anyone.

As he lays her back onto the bed, she playfully tugs at his jeans, and offers small pecks across his chest in hopes to distract him.

Though, he needs no distraction, Sean allows her to continue, knowing what she wants and he aches to give it to her, badly. Ruby, this beautiful, smart, sexy woman, can't get enough of him. It turns him on in ways he's never felt, because the truth is, he absolutely can't get enough of her.

When he's finally free of his clothing and she of hers, Sean uses his mouth to trace a wet, jagged line down her neck towards her breasts, stopping for a moment to squeeze and taste them. He then continues on his way towards her stomach, and then, down to the V of her hips.

Sean flickers little circles on her skin with his tongue as he licks her waist from one side to the other. She moans and arches her back beneath his touch, shivering every time his tongue tickles her bare skin. Mini seizures of pleasure overcome her and she grabs his head as his lips make their way further south.

Sean drives her crazy with desire as he focuses on the most sensitive area between her thighs over and over and over again. She gives in, hoping that he'll stop, but she finds herself wanting more as he playfully teases her.

Sean's warm, hard body slides upward to lay directly against hers. Without resting his entire weight on top of her, he supports himself with one arm and wraps her up in the other.

Warm air enters her ear as he whispers her name. Their eyes meet for the first time in minutes. She can't get over how quickly she'd fallen for him. It's as if they're destined to be. All of the anticipation up until this moment had her imagining how it would be, but now that they're here, there's nothing that could've prepared her for this.

The way move they together so slowly and gently is like a calm current against a beautiful lonely beach. Their rhythms are in concert with each other while they moan from deep within. He holds her slender hands tight within his as they continue to move in tandem, breathing deeply.

The feeling of her warmth and moistness surrounding him is ecstasy on a level he's never experienced before. His heartbeat quickens as he feels every pulse tighten and strengthen around him.

Sean can hold back no longer. He waits until his love is on the brink of satisfaction before he joins her in an explosive conclusion to the most magical, most marvelous lovemaking he's ever known.

Moments later, Ruby collapses onto the damp sheets, wet with the remanence of their hot passionate love. Sean joins her as the they try catching their breath in disbelief that they'd finally done it. They'd finally allowed themselves to be free to be together, free of feelings of guilt or regret.

Ruby snuggles next to him and rests her head on the top of his chest.

"I'm so glad I found you," she says sleepily. "I've been waiting for you my whole life and I don't ever want to let you go."

Sean smiles. He kisses her on the top of her head. She twirls her fingers in his chest hair for a few seconds before finally falling asleep.

An hour later, Sean is still awake. He lies there watching her, grateful that God has given him a chance to finally be with someone who's worth having his heart. More than anything he could have ever imagined, the love he feels is stronger than anything he'd felt for anyone in his past. More than he'd ever felt for Pam.

Sean cradles her a little tighter as he fantasizes about their perfect future together: dinner dates in Manhattan, museum visits, and long walks in Central Park. Perhaps weekend trips to Atlantic City, or Ocean City, Maryland, or maybe they could plan a full vacation to anywhere they want to go in the world. He'd always wanted to visit Bangkok.

Wherever life takes them, as long as they're together, there's no other place he'd rather be. He continues to watch her chest rise and fall beneath the thin sheets as she inhales and exhales.

Suddenly, a sinking feeling falls over him. A cloud of darkness shrouds his fantasies until his thoughts are completely blank. Scully's voice intrudes in the deepest pockets of his mind as flashbacks of Sean's meeting with him and the other men spin forward. Fear rides in on the coattails of his fantasies.

His breathing and heart rate quicken and Ruby stirs, feeling the slightest change in her comfort from lying on his chest. He prays she doesn't awaken.

His stomach begins to twist in knots. Anxiety rises from the pit of his stomach with the heat of fire and it settles within the base of his throat.

What am I thinking? We can never do any of these things with people trying to kill us! They, whoever they are,

are gonna keep hunting us down until we're both dead. We'll never be able to live a normal life unless this hit is canceled. But how? How can I call off a hit if I can't confirm who's behind it? All signs point to Tony because of Mike but, what if I'm wrong? What if it's someone else?

Sean continues to ponder possible solutions. The more sensible thing to do would be to tell Scully the truth. He could tell him where to find Ruby and that way he'd be sure that she would be home, safe with her family. *But how do I explain why we're at David's house? How to I explain to Scully that I know his daughter, that I love his daughter?*

And how do I explain to Ruby that I work for her real father, a man she doesn't even know?

Sheila's reluctance to call her aunt herself doesn't seem so unreasonable now. As more thoughts spin around in his head, the reality settles in that Ruby's life truly is in imminent danger. He can think of only one option to ensure she's kept safe and out of harm's way. He'd worry about his own well-being later. He can handle these streets but Ruby, sweet Ruby, she just isn't built for this life.

He pushes the thought out of his mind as he desperately tries to find just one more solution. Anything to keep from having to do what he fears will cause her the most pain.

How can I keep Ruby safe without her finding out about her dad, without her finding out about me? I won't work for Scully anymore, that's for sure. I refuse be his protégé or whatever the hell it was that he called me. Next in line, I think. I just want to be as far away from everything and everyone as possible, just me and Ruby living a peaceful life, a long and safe peaceful life.

The only problem is that Scully also wants to do the same with Ruby. He wants out of this homegrown empire he's built and he wants to take Ruby with him too.

Sean glances down at her again. He needs to protect her but how? He can't do it here. If they found out where Sheila lived, they could just as easily find David, right? Would they be that stupid to come looking for them at a cop's house?

The more he ruminates, the harder and more painful his decisions become. *She said she didn't ever want to let me go.* And neither does he. A lump tightens in his throat.

His eyelids begin to burn with tears and his chest tightens as he finally settles on a decision. If Ruby hates him enough, she'll never want to see his face again. Maybe then she'll leave and go home for good making it impossible for her father's enemies to find her. Scully will have to call off the search once she's back home and safe.

He swallows hard and exhales heavily. He looks at her once again and bends down to gently kiss her lips. The lips he'd dreamt of kissing, of the woman who'd stolen his heart. He already regrets his decision. Sean quietly gets dressed, and hovers over her for minutes watching her slumber.

He knows what he has to do. He walks towards the door and opens it, looking back one last time, and slowly shuts it behind him. In order for Ruby to hate him enough to go back home, he will have to abandon any chance of a life with her, forever. How quickly his dream died, the sheets barely dry from their lovemaking. She'll hate him for sure, he thinks. And she'll have every reason to. But he meant every word he said, he just didn't think about their safety in the heat of the moment.

As he quietly makes his way down David's stairs, he can't help but think how ironic it is that he, Sean, is essentially doing to Ruby what Scully did to her and her mother all those years ago.

But his love is too strong to be selfish and put her in harm's way. The only way Ruby can survive is if a piece of him dies too. Maybe Scully's right, Sean realizes. Maybe they're more alike than he thought.

Chapter 6

Jerome kills the engine in his driveway. He sits there knowing that as soon as he walks into the house, Marcia will want to know how his conversation with Cassius went.

He hadn't spoken to his wife for a couple of days. He'd been away at a seminar in California with his colleagues to learn about a new drug that had recently been approved by the FDA to treat a type of cancer he specializes in. His days were fully booked but to be honest, he could've made time for her. Anything was better than being at home at this point.

The time difference did make it difficult to reach her, although she probably would've stayed up all night to take his call. There always seemed to be a convenient conflict in their schedules. Well, his schedule. He can hear her saying it now.

Jerome mentally prepares himself to be persecuted by his wife. She has a lot of pent-up anger and had no one to take it out on. So many thoughts run through his head.

He tried to call Ruby a few times while he was away but received no answer. Why isn't she picking up? Sheila hadn't answered either and that made him even more suspicious because she's the more level headed one.

Jerome enters the house to find Marcia in the entertainment room drinking a cup of tea. As he approaches her, he quickly realizes the error in his ways. His wife looks as if she hadn't slept in days. He stands directly in front of her but she appears not to see him.

"Marcia," he says quietly. He waits for her to reply. No answer.

"Marcia," he says again.

She slowly sips from her mug of steaming peppermint tea and finally brings herself to look at him.

"Jerome?"

"I'm home," he replies.

She cuts her eyes at him.

"I can see that," she says. "Is Ruby with you?"

He can tell she's being sarcastic. Barely wanting to answer her question, he takes a deep breath.

"No," he sighs.

Marcia shakes her head and fixates on the herbs floating in the steaming hot liquid in her mug.

"Well, I hope you didn't think I was gonna jump for joy because *you're* finally home. Where the fuck is my child, Jerome?!" she screams. She slams her mug down on the table, spilling tea everywhere. She rises from the couch and paces the room.

"Do you know where she is? Huh? I've been walking around this house worried sick and I don't know what's going on. I told you to do something about it but I don't know *what* you're doing. You're off at some damn seminar, working, when my baby could be God knows where with God knows who!"

"Marcia, I was working, I'm sorry. I couldn't just not go! I was a freaking keynote speaker! How would it look if I just didn't show up?"

Marcia spins around on her heels. She glares a hot scathing hole into him.

"How would that look?" she snaps. "How would it look if the coroner is pulling the sheet back from our daughter's face?" she yells.

"Marci, how can you even say that?"

"How could *you* even say the shit you just said? You have some nerve, Jerome, you know that? All I've been thinking about these past few days is, is my baby okay, and is she safe? Who has her and why can't she call home? And *you're* thinking about *work*?!"

Marcia tries to get a breath in between her words. Fury builds inside of Jerome.

"Marci, didn't you go to work too? Huh? Didn't you have meetings that you couldn't miss? I had to do what I had to do. I still have to support this family and-"

"What family, Jerome?" Marcia opens her arms and

spins in the center of the room. "What family do we have without her?" She cries. "I'm trying to be strong to keep my sanity, but I don't know how much more of this I can take."

"Baby, I love Ruby too. I thought about her every single day, I called and called and I didn't get an answer either, so don't think that I'm just out here working and I could care less about her!"

"So, what did you do about it, Jerome? What?"

Jerome takes a seat on the couch where his wife sat moments earlier. He massages the tension out of his temples.

"I called Cassius…"

"And?" She stands in front of him, watching, holding her breath.

"And I told him everything about how Ruby has been acting lately and how she just up and left to New York and we haven't heard from her since."

"So, what's he gonna do?"

"He said he's gonna send out a few of his guys to find her and put her under surveillance so he knows where she is," he explains.

"Surveillance," Marcia says. "Why would he do that? He probably told everyone who she is! Doesn't that man get it?"

"Get what?" he asks.

Marcia throws up her hands in frustration.

"You know what Jerome? You lost control of this situation the minute Ruby heard him on that antiquated answering machine I told you to get rid of years ago! You and Cassius are both alike you know that? Doing things, the old way. Cassius doesn't understand how his mouth gets him into trouble. How trusting everyone puts himself and others in danger. How in the world did a complete stranger know that we were having dinner at Patricia's house, Jerome? I've said it a hundred times before and I'll say it again! People just don't know that kind of information unless they were told! I know for a fact we weren't followed that night because we always watched our backs! They knew where we were gonna be and at what time. Someone close to him had to know. That was an inside job. Cassius wouldn't believe me then, and apparently he still doesn't cause he done told *everyone* how to find my daughter!"

"Marci, I don't think it went down like that."

"Of course, you wouldn't cause you're just as dumb as he is. You men, I swear! Where is she at, does he know yet?"

Jerome looks away.

"I told him to check at Sheila's house first and to call us and tell us if she was there. Then we'd would come and get her."

"Why the hell couldn't we just go out there ourselves Jerome? I don't get it!"

He watches her pace and carefully thinks about what he's going to say next.

"Because we don't want to scare her if she knows anything. We'll just be admitting that we're trying to hide something from her if we run out there like the world is about to end. She'll want to know why she can't stay, especially if she's just *visiting* Sheila."

"She's gonna have to come home because, I *said* so!" Marcia screams, becoming more and more unhinged by the minute.

"Marci, she's 21! You can't just go out there and drag her back home because you *say* so!"

"So how are we supposed to do it when Cassius calls and tells us where she's at?"

Jerome tries to think of a way to retrieve his daughter without exposing their past. He's at a loss for words.

"I don't know," he whispers. His heart sinks. He thought he had it all figured out but now as he says it aloud, he realizes that he hadn't.

"I know one thing," Marcia says.

"What?"

She grabs her coat and her purse.

"I'm going to get my child."

"Marcia, where are you going? You don't even know where to start looking!"

"I'm going to Sheila's and then I'm going to Pam's." She heads towards the door as Jerome calls out to her.

"I forgot to mention something, Marci."

"What is it?" she asks annoyed as she searches her purse for her car keys.

"Cassius told me that he wants to get out of the business and he wants his family back."

"And what does that mean?" She asks terrified.

"He wants Ruby."

"NO! Absolutely not!"

Jerome walks towards her trying to comfort her. He knows he shouldn't have mentioned it but this is something he couldn't keep from her.

"Maybe it's time, baby. Maybe she should know about her father. He's changing now and he's, he's trying to live his life, the way he should have all those years ago. The man never had a chance to watch his daughter grow up."

"That's his own fault," she says as the tears finally spill from her eyes. Her throat tightens.

"Baby, everyone makes mistakes, we have to forgive and-"

"I don't have to forgive *him*, Jerome. He chose to live his life that way. *He* chose to throw away *everything* for that so called 'empire'. He didn't think twice..." she sobs. "He chose the drugs, the money, the bitches, and the power over me, over Ruby. How could he do that to us? How could he just tell us to leave and never come back like that? I loved him so much and it's like it didn't even matter to him. How was I supposed to raise my child on my own like that? I had no family. I had to leave them all behind for years until we were settled.

"My family didn't know where we were for *years*! I couldn't talk to my momma. I couldn't talk to my father. I didn't see my sisters and we used to be *so* close. He turned my whole world upside down and for what? So he could continue to keep selling his drugs and screwing his whores? He didn't care about me and he didn't care about Ruby, so why does he care about her now?"

"He did care about you," Jerome reassures her. His voice is stern, yet shaky. It is not easy to listen to his wife talk about the man she used to love, and it seems after all these years, Marcia is still just as hurt as she was the day Cassius sent her away.

"And he cared about Ruby—that's why he sent you out of state, so you could get away from anyone who was trying to hurt the two of you. That's why he sent me with you, to protect you and make sure nothing happened. Don't you see, Marci? He loved you more than anything in this world, and he loved Ruby because she was a product of your love. He had to give you up so you and Ruby could live! He did that for you!"

Marcia's eyes are weary. She has such *tired* eyes, Jerome observes. The longer she quietly stares at him, the more he realizes that she didn't hear a word he'd said. She was convinced, even after fifteen years, that Cassius loved his work more than he loved her or their daughter. And after so long, she tucked away her feelings for Cassius deep down inside and focused on the love she had for Ruby and the love she grew for Jerome.

Dealing with Ruby's awkward behavior and her recent disappearance awakened painful memories, including those of the death of her best friend and the sudden permanent separation from the man she used to love.

"Jerome, I still despise that man and there is no way in *hell* I'm going to let him come back into her life. No...way...in...hell!"

Marcia slams the door behind her and jumps into her car. She screeches out of the driveway and speeds out of sight. As she reaches the highway, she reminisces about Cassius and the life he threw away.

The night of her wedding, when she saw Cassius weaving his way through her guests in his chic tux, she felt something grip her heart from deep within. She couldn't describe it. Perhaps she refused to admit it but what she felt was a longing inside of her. A longing that made her want to feel his touch one last time. She wanted him to hold her in his strong arms and finally, finally apologize for *everything*. Everything he'd done to her, to her family and most importantly, to their daughter.

Marcia remembers wishing she was able to turn back time. If she could, she would stay and fight. She would never leave her parents, her sisters, and her friends. Maybe she could've presented a more convincing argument for him to put their family first and leave the game for good. No, she thought. She's convinced that if given the chance, all would be for nothing. He would do it all over again because that's the kind of selfish jerk he is. He's a selfish, murdering jerk who deserves to burn in hell.

She shakes the thought of them together from her head. He had an entrancing effect on her and she hated it. She hated it because it prevented her from seeing the truth about him. She'd been so blinded by love and lust that she'd often overlooked the cruel, ruthless, unforgiving monster that he was. This man killed people, with his own hands. She had, at one point, watched him shoot someone at point-blank range because they'd cost him money. It was a dangerous life he lived, and though she hated it, she loved him too much to live without him. That is, until the day he sent her away.

She even carried a small handgun on her for protection because he'd insisted on it. Cassius may have been revered by many of his colleagues, but no one got to his position without making a few enemies along the way. She had to protect herself and the life of her baby girl.

She's not proud of it, but the haunting memories of her discharging her weapon, a few more occasions than she'd like to admit, plays like a silent movie in her mind.

Marcia speeds onto the highway with only her thoughts to haunt her. Fifteen years ago, she never truly realized how awful he was for her. how dangerous he could be. Her devout Christian parents saw right through Cassius like a missing pane in their stained-glass window. From the moment they'd made his acquaintance, the relationship between Marcia and her parents was never the same. She remembers it like it was yesterday.

There she was, 20 years old and 6 months pregnant with Ruby. She shook like a young gazelle in the midst of a lion pride at the thought of revealing her "condition" to her parents. But there was no way around it. She couldn't hide her growing belly much longer. Marcia's mother has always been known as having a much calmer disposition than her strict bishop husband, but that disposition was nowhere to be found the day her mother suspected that she was pregnant.

Marcia's father took one look at Cassius' gold chains, Kangol hat, and white-on-white Adidas sneakers and judged him, immediately.

"And who is this? Is this the boy that done got you knocked up?!"

"This is Cassius, Daddy."

Cassius extended his hand in respect, honored to shake the hand of the most respected minister in Jamaica, Queens. Bishop Matthews' left eye began to twitch at the sight of the ghastly, gaudy gold rings and bracelets Cassius adorned on each hand. Her father rejected the hand of "the devil," as he called him, almost certain his skin would singe at the touch of him.

Marcia knew bringing him by the house was a big mistake. She tried to prep him on what he should wear, what he should say, how he should behave, but he refused every ounce of her advice.

"If I can't be myself, what's the point? I respect your father as a pillar of this community, but I'm not changing who

I am because you'd rather your parents believe a lie. He'll either accept me for who I am, or he won't accept me at all. And I'm fine with that. It won't change the way I feel about you. Nothing will."

Marcia was furious with him but she had to respect his decision. It didn't mean she didn't suffer from mini anxiety attacks the closer they got to the day of their family "meet and greet." She tried to put it off for as long as possible but she couldn't wait any longer. Just a week earlier, her mother had cornered her in the living room just as she walked through the front door.

"You think wearing baggy clothes and door knocker earrings from the avenue makes you look like Salt-N-Pepa? Well, it don't! It makes you look pregnant, in my house, under my roof and you'd better start explaining yourself before your father gets home because I can assure you, it's gonna be *a lot* worse."

Her sisters Tammy, Felicia, and Melina peeked from behind corners to eavesdrop while trying to remain quiet and unseen. They'd come home for Mother's Day to spend time with their parents and their youngest sister Marcia, whom they hadn't seen much of lately. She always had an excuse and claimed to be so busy, but they never knew what she was busy doing.

Marcia was the last one to leave the nest because she had a sweet deal with her parents. She could stay for as long as she liked, rent free, as long as she didn't end up like her sisters: young, pregnant, and unmarried. Their Christian household had seen its fair share of scandals over the past few years as two of Marcia's sisters had experienced the same fate. Melina had gotten pregnant with a handsome baby boy she named Michael and a year later, Tammy conceived a precious baby girl she named Sheila, their mother's middle name.

Although the Matthews household held two new, innocent, beautiful lives, the tension in the home grew to atomic levels. It mattered not that their granddaughter bore the namesake of the matriarch of the family. There was to be no fornicating and living in sin of any kind under their roof.

The family dynamic had become so toxic, both Melina and Tammy moved out and into a small apartment together. And even though Marcia's middle sister Felicia hadn't gotten pregnant, she too, left. She couldn't bear to live with her parents any longer and subject herself to listening to them speak such filth against her sisters. Felicia fled, fast on her sisters' heels, leaving a young Marcia behind to deal with them all alone.

The sisters pitied Marcia as they quickly grew

accustomed to their new and guilt-free way of living. Their freedom and independence was priceless and the support of each other was invaluable. But, there was one thing that made it almost impossible to find complete happiness—the youngest of them was still imprisoned in an oppressive, rule-laden household. They empathized immensely with her suffering.

The hurt in their mother's voice, when she discovered her youngest baby had fallen victim to the same fate as her oldest daughters, shook the walls of their family home like a crashing sea wall behind her beloved Moses. The cries and pleading from Marcia to her mother for forgiveness shattered her sisters' hearts and resurrected old and buried wounds as they listened to every filthy description of "Jezebel," as their mother called Marcia. According to their mother, they had become a family of Jezebels.

Melina, especially, suffered in silence from the brutal tongue lashing her little sister endured. Being the closest to Marcia, the two were inseparable. They were best friends. They shared everything with each other. Marcia even cried in her arms when her pregnancy test came back positive. Neither of them knew the best approach to telling their parents. Clearly, neither she nor Tammy had mastered that.

Marcia was devastated by the news of her pregnancy.

She feared the disappointment of her parents more than death, but it was her sister Melina who gave her the strength to approach them. It was Melina who gave her the support and encouragement to state her peace and to move on.

"Life *will* go on," Marcia remembers her saying. "It may seem like the end of the world in your moment of truth, but just know there is no better feeling than standing in it," Melina once told her.

It was in that moment when Marcia accepted her fate. She would plan to tell her parents about her baby on her own terms. Unfortunately, Mrs. Matthews' intuition and prior experiences with her daughters was stronger than Marcia's willingness to face the truth.

To watch their mother approach Marcia before she'd found the nerve to tell her parents on her own was difficult to witness. Marcia sobbed and pleaded with her mother not to tell their father, and it was unbearable to hear. Melina cried beside the others behind the kitchen wall. All three sisters knew that familiar pain all too well.

When their father came home from cleaning the church after a successful Mother's Day service, Marcia was forced to tell her father that she too would become a mother in a few months. Bishop Matthews took the news as expected. After what felt like hours of yelling, crying, scripture quoting, holy water tossing, Melina had finally had enough and jumped in to save her sister from further torment.

"Why don't we try something different this go-round? Clearly, condemning Marcia to hell for doing what is natural is not going to fix anything. The only thing it *will* do is run her away. Kind of like what you did to us."

Tammy and Felicia emerged from the kitchen and stood in solidarity beside them.

"How about you actually *meet* the father of Ce Ce's baby and get to know him. Give them *both* a chance. You don't have to continue to ruin our family every time we start one of our own."

After much deliberation, surprisingly their parents agreed, reluctantly. Imagine Marcia's horror when Cassius refused to dress appropriately to meet them for the first time. She remembered her sister's advice, to stand in her own truth. How can she force the man she loved, not to stand in his?

Bishop Matthews struggled to suppress his natural instinct to slap Cassius on the forehead with extra virgin olive oil and rebuke him in the name of Jesus. None of the answers Cassius gave to the bishop's intrusive questions were good enough. He sounded uneducated, egotistical, unrealistically optimistic, yet mild tempered. Even though Marcia's father persisted in his inquisition on Cassius' faith and lifestyle,

Cassius endured.

After Marcia left home and moved in with Cassius, Cassius told her that although he may not be the smartest man, or the savviest, there is only one thing he felt confident about, and that was his undying love for her and their unborn baby. He'd walk through fire if it meant that she would be standing at the end of it, waiting for him.

She believed him. In fact, she kept believing him throughout the years, although, admittedly it was a struggle. She struggled through every missed birthday, missed holiday and missed family dinners, while he was away in another country doing God knows what. She struggled through it all, but what she struggled with the most was his endless infatuation with other women. She remembers the time when she drew her own weapon on a girl she'd known from around town.

On this particular occasion, she'd gone to the project development where Cassius had grown up, to find him. His old stomping grounds were always teeming with activity, especially in the summer months. If she couldn't find him at home, she was sure she could find him there. Cassius could usually be found sitting with old men, playing chess on the concrete chess tables in the project's park or boasting about gang hits to the young boys in the area.

But on this day, the old men played chess alone. The group of girls usually posted up by the gate was one hood rat short and Marcia had a sneaky suspicion about where she was. Instead of leaving, she went into the building to one of his "boy's" apartments and found the bedroom door locked. He only slept there when he had late business to take care of, but it was still daylight. There was no way he should've been inside on a beautiful day like that. After knocking a couple of times, she pulled out her gun, shot the lock off the handle and walked right in. The girl was still mounted on top of him with the sheets wrapped around her waist.

She was naked from the bottom up and Marcia couldn't believe what she was seeing. She aimed the gun at the girl's head, shooting in her direction a few times and missing before Cassius convinced her to put the gun away. He didn't convince her, nor did he try to stop her from beating on the girl. He played it cool, lighting a cigar while watching the two women fight. When his mistress screamed to him for help, he just sat there and smiled.

"You knew who I was with when you dropped them panties. And you knew who my lady was too before you topped me off. So now you're getting your tail whopped," he laughed. "Ain't karma a –?"

Marcia forgave him soon after he begged and pleaded

with her to stay with him. He promised he wouldn't do it again, but after busting him time and time again, she decided to deal with it as long as he came home to her and their unborn child every night. It was a horrible time in her life. She could barely look at herself in the mirror. How could she face herself? What would her mother say if she could see her now?

Jerome on the other hand felt sorry for her. Somehow, being Cassius' best friend and partner, *he* always found the time to be there to console her, to talk her out of doing something stupid. Something Cassius made a low-level priority. Jerome had taken a liking to her and came around often, mostly for stimulating intellectual conversation as the two had much in common. He was sweet, which was the complete opposite of Cassius. He was book smart and anyone could tell that he had a bright future ahead of him. But he still possessed the same ignorant street mentality as Cassius and it was that which kept him from pursuing his dreams.

Jerome was Cassius' right-hand man and best friend who followed him almost everywhere he went. But there were times when Jerome didn't need to be present during certain transactions and trips abroad. He used *that* time to keep Marcia company, bringing them closer as friends.

Yet there was another problem. Patricia. Marcia's closest friend since childhood confided in her that she was secretly falling for Jerome. She couldn't stop talking about how handsome, how sweet, and how smart he was, about how different he was from the other guys in their hood. Marcia couldn't blame her. These were all things that attracted her to him as well, but she couldn't bring herself to stand in the way of Patricia's happiness. With so many failed relationships behind her, her good friend Patricia deserved to be happy.

After distancing herself from Jerome to allow Patricia to pursue and eventually capture his heart, Marcia and Jerome's friendship weakened and became distant. Distant enough for her to plummet into a depression with only her daughter Ruby to keep her sane.

Marcia weeps all the way to New York as her past flashes between each red light and highway toll. Her daughter is missing and forces unknown are trying to take her from her. Even Cassius wants Ruby for himself and Jerome…Jerome is just so lost. His behavior is unusual, more unusual than it's ever been since she's known him. She quickly dries her eyes.

"If you need something done, you have to do it yourself," she says aloud as she approaches an exit twenty miles off course from her destination. She detours towards the city, recklessly weaving in and out of traffic. There's someone she needs to speak to. Hopefully they're home.

Chapter 7

Ruby stretches her body, extending her arms wide to the feel the cool empty space beside her. Eyes still closed, she rubs against the cool sheets like a waking cat, waiting to touch an arm or leg not her own.

Feeling only the wrinkles in the linen beneath her fingertips, she narrowly opens her eyes to discover that she is indeed alone. She scans the unfamiliar room in search for him.

As she rises, she notices her panties in a bunch at the foot of the bed. A sleepy smile slowly stretches across her face as she remembers how Sean removed them and passionately made love to her all night.

She dresses quickly to meet everyone downstairs only to find Sheila and David in the middle of a passionate kiss in the kitchen.

"Ahem."

They separate, laughing at each other as they pretend to have something else important to do. Ruby rolls her eyes, amusingly shaking her head. They remind her of her parents.

My parents, she remembers. She hadn't spoken to her parents in days! She saw their missed calls but it was never a good time to speak to them. Plus, she didn't know what to say. They had to know that she was okay, right?

"Hey Rube, how was your sleep?" Sheila asks. Ruby blushes at the mention of it.

"Uh huh, I knew it!" Sheila says excitedly. "You got some, didn't you?"

"Sheila!" Ruby yells, nodding her head towards David.

"Girl, we all grown up in here, ain't no need to be shy."

"Well maybe she doesn't want you all up in her business," says David. Sheila always amuses him with how raw she is about *everything*. It's as if anything that comes to mind, just slides right out of her mouth.

"Look, I slept well, that's all I have to say," Ruby tries not to smile, still feeling a way about what happened last night.

"How *well* did yah sleep?" Sheila arches an eyebrow. Hoping to make a truce using her killer humor.

Ruby barely giggles. She pauses.

"*Very* well." They laugh, ready to put last night, behind them.

Girls. One minute they're enemies, the next it's like nothing even happened, David thinks as he flips through pages of the New York Times.

"So, speaking of the handsome devil, where is he?" Sheila asks.

"I don't know. I woke up and he wasn't there. I thought he was in the bathroom or something," replies Ruby.

"Nah," Sheila answers, "I was just in there. Maybe he went to the store or something."

"But he doesn't know any stores around here." Ruby looks outside. "I guess he may have just stepped out for a minute like you said. Maybe he went for a walk since his car is still in the driveway."

David glances up from his paper. He locks eyes with Sheila trying to communicate what he doesn't have the heart to say out loud.

"Well, never mind that girl. He'll be back sooner or later. How about some pancakes? You want eggs with that or what?" Sheila says, quickly moving on.

"Eggs are fine." Ruby sits down at the table and scrolls through her phone. "You know my mom and dad have been calling me."

"They've been calling me too."

"Did you answer them?" Ruby asks.

"No, 'cause I didn't want to talk to them before you did. Have you spoken to them yet?"

"No, I don't know what to say to them."

"Just tell them you're all right, Rube. They've gotta be worried about you." Sheila places the plates in front of Ruby and David and walks back to the stove. Without facing Ruby, she says, "As a matter of fact, you should probably just go home anyway."

As if the air has been sucked out of the room, Ruby's face loses just a bit of color.

"Go home? We still haven't solved the case," she glances between Sheila and David. "We still don't know what's going on! What about my mother...what about..."

"Ruby, *your* mother is at home, right now, as we speak, worried sick about you. She needs you and you need her more than you know."

"But I can call her right now and tell her that I'm fine, see?" She picks up the phone and starts to dial.

"Ruby, it's deeper than that. You need to be with your parents."

"But what about the *case*?!" she yells.

Sheila sighs. They'd just put this all behind them, or so she'd hoped. Now they're back at it again and she doesn't think she can relive another round of what'd happened last night. David sets the newspaper down on the table.

"Ruby, this case is becoming more and more dangerous the closer we get to finding out what really happened. For some reason, you guys have become targets and we don't know who it is or where it's coming from.

That's why we had to leave the house in such a hurry last night.

"When we first started this, I didn't think it would put you in harm's way, because it was such an old case. That's why I allowed you and Sheila to work together with me on it. But, last night...last night just proved that I made a huge mistake and I never should've allowed you two to get involved."

"But this is *our* case, David. We brought it to *you*! All you did was just dig it up!" Ruby shouts. "I can't believe my ears. This case means way more to me than it does to either of you. You don't have anything to lose, whereas I do! This would clear my mother of any connection to that murder! This would save my family and our reputation. I'm pretty sure Pam is *definitely* plottin' some shit now, especially after she'd already tried to *kill* me! That's why I need to get ahead of it and solve the case as quickly as possible. I need to be there every step of the way!"

"Ruby, I understand how you feel and I'll keep all of that in mind as I work the case which would've made it to my desk, eventually. This is what I do. I the captain, but I solve cases, too."

"Well, you're not doing a very good job at it, now are you?!" Ruby snaps.

"Ruby!" Sheila shouts.

David waves her down.

"It's okay, Sheila. It's okay. She's right. I'm not very good at it because if I was, I wouldn't have put you in danger in the first place. I should have stuck to protocol, thanked you for the information you'd given me, sent you away and gotten the whole department involved. And you wouldn't have had the slightest clue about what was going on."

He glares at Ruby, sick of her immaturity and recklessness. His voice grows stern as the last of his fleeting patience disappears.

"I risked my badge for you. I risked my *entire* career, my life, and I went against my oath to serve and protect, for you. I have placed you *and* Sheila in danger and I can no longer live with that. You're right. I haven't been doing a very good job. So, in order for me to do it better; I'm going to tell you that you can no longer be a part of this. You have to go home, now."

Silence. Sheila had no idea how David was going to convince Ruby to go home. She had no clue he even had that in him. Ruby on the other hand never expected David to speak to her that way. She'd always felt in control of all of this, until now.

"David, I'm sorry. I didn't mean to say-"

"Ruby, just call your parents now and tell them that you're on your way home. I'll take you myself." Ruby looks at Sheila. There's nothing Sheila can do now. This is for her own good.

"What about my car, Sheila? They're gonna ask about my car." Ruby is cornered. She's desperately trying to find a reason to stay, but they'd thought of everything.

"We'll tell them the alternator blew or something and it's getting fixed." Ruby stares at her phone. She really didn't want to call her parents but she has no choice. They're making her *leave*. But wait! Maybe Sean can make them change their minds. He'll fight for her to stay, she knows it! After last night, after the things he'd said, he would never let her go!

"What about Sean," she asks?

"What about him?" says David.

"He still hasn't come back yet and I'm not leaving without seeing him. Besides he wouldn't want me to go."

"Ruby, please...stop fighting it," Sheila pleads.

"I'm calling him to see where he is," Ruby says, not giving up without a fight. She paces the room, with Sheila and David's eyes following her. She dials Sean's number once, twice, three times. By the fourth time, defeat sweeps over her and her heart sinks.

"Call *home*," says Sheila, impatient with her stubborn

113

cousin.

Ruby, frustrated yet defeated selects her step-fathers contact in her phone and he answers on the second ring.

"Ruby, baby, where are you?! Why haven't you called us? Are you okay, are you...are you hurt? What's going on?"

"Jerry, Jerry, I'm okay. I'm with Sheila and we're at a friend's house."

"Why haven't you called? Why have you been ignoring us? Your mother is worried *sick* about you! She's going crazy?! How dare you put us through this! What the hell is wrong with you?"

Tears form in her eyes. There's so much she can't say, but she never meant to make them worry the way they did.

"Young lady I'm waiting for an *answer* from you!"

"I'm sorry, Dad. I was just so busy..."

"Don't you *Dad* me! You only call me Dad when you want me to go easy on you. What were you so busy doing, huh? What was so important that you couldn't call?!"

She's never heard him like this before, not even during the worst fights between him and her mother, and he had some nerve. She could be asking him tons of questions too!

"As a matter of fact," she replies, "If you really want to know, I've been so busy trying to figure out why you lied about the man who was on the answering machine! Why you

114

lied about where you were born and why all of a sudden you have some mysterious man pop up at the wedding who I've never seen come around before! And you think *I'm* the one acting weird?!"

Jerome is speechless. Marcia's right! Ruby *is* out there, digging to find the truth and all along he's been letting her run free, not realizing that she's trying to uncover his past.

"Ruby, what…what are you talking about?"

"Oh, you know good and well what I'm talking about!"

Sheila is frantically mouthing the word 'NO' and waving her hands. Ruby notices, but she couldn't care less. She's tired of the lies, tired of the betrayal from those who are closest to her. She's doing things on her own terms now.

"Ruby, you need to come home right now so we can talk or else I'm coming out there to get you and I'll bring you back myself. Where are you?"

"Like I said, I'm at a friend's house. Figure it out." She hangs up and flops back down into the chair at the table before her legs give out from beneath her.

"Ruby, what did you just do? Why did you *tell* him that!?" Sheila is aghast.

"Because, Shells, he was trying to make me feel as if all of this is my fault. As if I'm the one who's messed up, but he's the one hiding stuff, not me!"

"Ruby, how can you be so stupid? Your parents care about you! They only want what's best for you." Sheila rubs her temples, trying to suppress an oncoming migraine. She doesn't know what else to do.

"Did Sean talk to you last night, Ruby?" David asks out of curiosity, unsure if she understands the gravity of the situation.

"…about *what*?" Ruby snaps.

David stands up. "Never mind," he says sadly as he leaves the room.

"So, now what?" Sheila asks tossing her hands into the air. Her face is lined with worry. So much for their plan of trying to send her home.

"So now we find out who's after me and why," Ruby replies. Sheila sits down and looks into Ruby's eyes.

"I think its best that you sit down and talk with Sean. There is something he needs to tell you."

"He's not picking up."

"Well, text him."

Ruby begins to text.

SEAN, I TRIED TO CALL YOU A FEW TIMES. WHERE ARE YOU? SHEILA SAYS YOU HAVE SOMETHING TO TELL ME. PLEASE CALL ME.

Ruby and Sheila sit, waiting in silence for him to text back. Sheila's phone receives a few notifications and after a few quick glances, she shoves the phone back into her pocket. They continue to sit for over an hour before Sean finally replies back.

RUBY, I THOUGHT ABOUT EVERYTHING THAT HAPPENED LAST NIGHT AND I COULDN'T HAVE IMAGINED IT ANY OTHER WAY. BUT, I'M STRUGGLING WITH SOME THINGS RIGHT NOW AND I THINK IT'S BEST WE END THINGS RIGHT HERE. I'M SORRY.

Chapter 8

"Who does this li'l girl think she's talking to? Like I'm one of her li'l fuckin friends or something? Has she lost her got damn mind?! She doesn't understand." He yells aloud.

"She doesn't understand what's at stake or else she wouldn't be floating around Queens all carefree and shit!" Jerome tosses shoe box after shoe box onto an already cluttered floor.

"Of course, she doesn't understand. That's the whole point! She's not supposed to, but she thinks she can find answers to questions she doesn't even know yet?"

Another box falls to the floor.

"This is what we get. This is what we get for trying to protect her, for giving her…" he struggles as he reaches into the depths of his closet, "for giving her… a life others would kill for. *Die* for."

He opens a larger box, dusty with years of neglect, stuffed with outdated clothes, musty with the stench of mothballs and old cologne. No doubt from a bottle that had probably broken somewhere beneath.

"It's here…I *know* it's here." Jerome hops down from his stepladder and walks to the end of his walk-in closet, angrily yanking down more items from the shelf his wife designated for light storage.

"Dammit!" He stands in the middle of the floor, his eyes scanning the piles of mess before him one by one, hoping that he'd overlooked a bag or a box or something. He glances up towards the shelf from a new vantage point in the center of the room, and just like that, there it is.

Slipping on debris blocking his way, he races up the stepladder and stretches as far as he possibly can towards the back shelf to reach a black box. It's pushed so far back, he could barely read the inscription "JT's stuff" on it.

Jerome tosses the box onto the bed and enters a combination to unlock the contents inside. He thumbs through old passports with false names, fake IDs bearing his image, old airline ticket stubs to Cuba, Kuwait, China, and Singapore.

Singapore. A faded smile crosses his lips as he flips through the pages of his Singaporean passport, filled with overlapping stamps of proof of his exotic trips abroad. A tattered business card with a pin and phone number to a woman named Monica slips out from its pages. His eyes lose focus as he reminisces himself into a daze, fondly remembering his affairs with that mysterious woman and her all-female staff.

He shakes the thought from his mind and tosses the card to the side, determined to keep searching for one item in particular. He pulls out a few pictures, a couple of heavy gold chains and two ancient beepers, until his fingers graze the coolness of steel and a textured nylon-grip frame.

With a sigh of relief, Jerome gently lifts his .380 caliber semi-automatic pistol out of the box. He turns it over and over in his hands, feeling the light weight of the steel and admiring its mint condition.

"God, it's been a while and it still shines like new." The magazine lay separate and with one swift move, he inserts it and aims at his own reflection in the closet door mirror. Perfect form.

"Just like riding a bike." But something's off. He studies himself for a moment, holding his gun and shifting his stance. He's changed. His stethoscope is still in the pocket of the lab coat lying on the bed, and the teal scrubs he's wearing still have the day's stains from a surgery he'd performed earlier that afternoon.

"Jesus!" Everything he'd worked for up until this moment is at risk and the only way to protect it is to break an oath he'd taken both professionally and personally.

After a quick change of clothes, Jerome stuffs his pistol into the back pocket of his jeans and laces up his boots. He jumps into his black Audi and speeds towards the turnpike, right into bumper to bumper traffic.

"Come on!"

He had so much on his mind he'd forgotten about evening rush hour traffic! Not knowing which friends Ruby has all the way out in Queens, he has an idea where she might be from a stack of very expensive wedding photos. He hopes she's there when he arrives, whenever that may be.

****

Marcia pulls into an empty space, relieved to have finally found street parking only a five-minute walk from her destination. She'd been circling the area for nearly a half hour, cursing out the overabundance of pedestrians along the way, frustrated for even being in New York City in the first place.

A block and a half to Third Avenue between Sixty-Second and Sixty Third Streets, she repeats to herself. She locates the building she's looking for and a doorman politely ushers her inside to a glorious marble-floored, shimmering-gold lobby. As she approaches the front desk of this historical high-rise building, a wide-eyed concierge rushes to meet her, thrilled to see a beautiful, fresh, new face.

"Welcome to Sky Rise Lofts. If you're here, you're home. How may I assist you?"

"Hi, I'm looking to go to the 5th floor to see a Mr.

121

Cassius O' Neil."

Marcia smiles, trying to match his expression, but his eyes squint slightly.

"Is Mr. O' Neil expecting you, Ms...?"

"Marcia Greene and yes, we have an appointment today. You see, I am..." she hesitates. *What the hell am I?* She isn't prepared. She didn't realize he'd have a concierge! But as she thinks of it, *Of course*, he would. With enemies like his, she wouldn't be surprised if the doorman was packing heat.

He looks at her even more suspiciously now.

"I'm his, um..."

"Oh," he smiles shyly, "you must be his *Thursday* appointment." He whispers the day of the week as if it were a secret. His face blushes a slight light shade of rose. "You must be new. I haven't seen you around here before."

Marcia exhales.

"Just so you know, Mr. O' Neil wishes not to be called by his full name. Scully will do just fine, and you'll do well to remember that. Oh, and just so you don't have any trouble with the night guard, tell him that you're Mr. Scully's Thursday appointment and he'll send you right up. Okay?"

She's in shock. She has no idea what had just happened but she's not complaining. Marcia obviously hadn't had a plan to convince him to let her up. For once, Scully's penis does come in handy.

She grips her purse tightly for comfort. Not knowing what to expect, she stands in the center of the elevator, waiting to face her greatest fear: coming face to face with the one person who'd ruined her life. This realization ignites something that's been slumbering inside of her for a very long time. With a crack of her neck and a deep breath, she considers letting out what has been festering inside.

As the elevator rises, scenarios and repercussions play in her head, all of which would land her either in jail or in the electric chair.

If this city knew even half of what he's done, the Mayor would give me the fuckin key.

She continues upward; finally prepared to face him, to face her past, something she never imagined she'd do. If conquering one of her greatest fears would keep her daughter safe, then she'll do it, and he in turn would have to face *her* because there is no way in hell she is ever letting him near Ruby.

The freight elevator comes to a stop. It had taken her directly to the fifth floor and, it seems, right into the loft!

"Hello...hello...is anyone here?"

Marcia steps out and into a vast open space.

There's no answer. As she walks out further onto the floor, she realizes that she's standing inside a fully furnished lobby. There's a door with a peephole, which she assumes is the main door. It's large, heavy and made entirely of reclaimed wood.

Fancy.

She knocks firmly three times and waits for an answer. She knocks again, harder this time, and still no answer. She waits impatiently and nervously stuffs an envelope with Cassius' address on it into her purse and waits impatiently.

"Where is he?"

****

Terry emerges from the bathroom in her purple satin robe, towel-drying her hair. She smiles at the setting sun pouring in from the balcony window, just grateful for a little peace and quiet. Finally, she feels refreshed and relaxed. The past few nights had been extremely painful watching the man she loves pacing around the house, talking to himself and spending endless hours on the patio in the middle of the night.

It not only tore at her, it made her feel alone. In his misery, she was non-existent.

She hadn't known what the problem was until he exploded one day, telling her about how that kid Sean wanted to bail out on him in the middle of a job. She didn't understand why he was *so* angry. They both knew the day would come when Sean would want to leave. But what she didn't know was that Cassuis had an even larger, more important purpose for Sean, and that was to protect his daughter, Ruby.

No sooner than giving him the task, Cassius received a phone call from Sean telling him that he couldn't do it. He wanted out. He didn't give any explanations; he just hung up and never answered his phone again. Cassius lost his mind. The betrayal from a kid he'd grown to respect and nurture not only injured his pride but it reinforced his failure as a father.

What to say? She never even knew he *had* a daughter. What do you say to that? The only thing she could focus on was the most obvious question to her.

"How could you keep something so important from me? After all of these years, after all of the abortions I've had, you couldn't share with me the real reason why you didn't want any kids?" Terry remembers his face; pain and confusion etched within the folds of his furrowing brow.

"How is this about you, Terry? Why must you make this about *you*? Yes, I have a daughter and you're right, I didn't want any more children because they're a liability."

"A liability? Are you serious? Loving a child is the most beautiful, most precious thing in the world…"

"Don't you think I know that?!" Cassius snapped. "I love my daughter more than anything or anyone in this world. But even she's a liability! Do you know what they tried to do to me? To her?"

Terry was silent, still unsure of where he was going with this.

"They tried to kill us! They tried to kill *her*! Whoever *they* are, they knew she was my weakness. They knew that I would be vulnerable if anything ever happened to her. Emotionally defenseless for an ultimate takeover. But I outsmarted them, me and…" His voice trailed off.

"I can't get past something you said about this "ultimate" takeover," Terry interjected. "So, you did what? Left your daughter so that you could have all of *this*?"

"I did it so that *she* could have all of this. All of this is for her!"

"Are you sure?" Terry reads him for the truth she believes he's hiding behind. "You know what I think? I think you're addicted to this and you try to make yourself feel better by projecting your noble actions onto those who you've hurt."

"Good thing I didn't ask you *what you think.* Somehow as I'm trying to figure this out, trying to find a way to make sure my daughter is safe, you make this about us. And I want there to be an 'us,' Terry." He grabs her hands. "But I can't focus on that right now. I need to focus on my daughter and I can't do that here."

Terry sat worrying about him throughout the night. He'd left her sitting hurt and alone in that large, lonely apartment. After hours of sulking, she finally decided that she couldn't be any help to him if she were depressed as well. A long hot shower, freshly washed hair and a relaxed mind is all she needed. Hopefully, a clear head will help her to find a solution for Cassius before he does something he'll regret.

She dries her hair and walks towards the kitchen to make a cup of tea. Loud knocks on the front door echo throughout the loft. She hadn't heard it before. Not over the running shower but now its deafening. She peers through the peephole to see a woman standing there with her head down. Terry backs up and heads to the closet to retrieve her gun.

"Who is it?" she yells.

Marcia's caught off guard. Is that a woman's voice? Is he seeing someone? Someone permanent? No. She could be another Thursday appointment. But, that doesn't make any sense unless she's left over from Wednesday, then..." her mind begins to spin.

"I said, who is it?!"

Marcia shakes off her overanalytical thoughts.

"I'm Scully's Thursday appointment," she replies.

"Oh really, I wasn't aware he was still having those," says Terry. She stands to the side of the door, gripping her gun in both hands.

Did Cassius really book another girl without telling me? I know he's stressed but what the hell! He said he ain't need no one else but me! So, who the hell is this?!

"May I come in?"

Terry pauses a few moments.

The locks and deadbolts slowly unlatch. The door opens but there's no one to greet Marcia. She proceeds to enter with caution.

"Don't move," Terry slams the door behind her. She emerges from behind Marcia, slowly. One quick glance at her and Terry can tell she's a woman well into her 40s, cover-girl beautiful with stunning features, but her eyes are dark, troubled, and piercing.

Now I know this bitch is a damn lie. Cassius don't pick em this old.

"Who are you?" Terry asks threateningly.

The longer the woman stands in silence, the more Terry's blood boils. It's as if this woman isn't afraid of anything.

Marcia struggles to maintain control over her rising temper. Of all of the things she wants to do right now, her first priority is to get answers. She has no choice but to speak. At this point, the woman in her tiny, purple, satin robe, can pull the trigger before she would be able to do anything about it.

"My name is Marcia and like I said, I'm here for my Thursday…"

"You're a lying ass bitch! You ain't here for no "Thursday appointment". You're too old, Mar-ci-a. Scully wouldn't blink an eye at you."

Marcia shakes her head. Just as she'd expected—Cassius hadn't changed a bit. Still up to his old antics and now he has whores for every day of the week. And by the looks of this one holding the gun, she must…live here?

Marcia examines her from where she stands, making note of every detail without shifting her ever-observant eyes. She's pretty, yes, but in no way a comparison to herself. Her wet hair drenched the entire top half of her thin robe, revealing she was wearing nothing beneath it; she had to have just gotten out of the shower.

"Now I'm gonna ask you again," Terry takes the safety

off. "Who are you and what are you doing here?"

"My name *is* Marcia, but you're right. I'm not another one of Cassius' whores…"

"Did you call him by his name?!"

"I'll call him whatever I damn well please!" Marcia challenges.

"Why are you here? Huh? How did you find this place?" Terry, more nervous than she'd like to admit, wipes her brow, denying it's probably more sweat than water.

She refuses to take her eyes off of Marcia.

"Look, I have something in my bag that will help me explain but, I need to speak with him, it's very urgent," says Marcia. Her movements are slow while she fingers at the opening of her purse.

"Don't move or I swear to God…" the gun shakes in Terry's hands. She wipes her forehead again with the sleeve of her robe.

I don't know who this woman is but, she must really want to die tonight.

"Just let me pass you this envelope. That's all, and then you'll understand." Marcia says, sounding calmer than she feels.

Terry snatches the crumpled envelope from Marcia and pulls out an old transfer statement. She can't hide the shock on her face even if she tried. She thought she knew everything about Cassius, but this doesn't make sense. She's seen this account number before. Over and over again while she handled finances for Cassius in the past. But why does Marcia have this statement?

"How did you know where to find him?" Terry asks, still glancing over the sheet of paper.

A familiar click releases the safety from Marcia's gun. Terry stares down the barrel, inches from her face.

Fuck!

She'd made herself vulnerable. Upper hand, gone.

"He's the father of my child. I always know where to find him. Now, drop your gun and take a few steps back."

Terror fills Terry instantly.

"Pulling a gun on me was the worst thing you could've done," says Marcia. "I haven't slept in five fucking days, I'm delirious and my child is missing. I can't even think straight and everything I know, my entire life, is falling apart right in front of me," her voice trembles. "My child has been missing for days and I want her back now! I came here for Cassius and to get some answers and what do I get but you pointing a *gun* in my face!"

Marcia rushes Terry. After a few quick heavy handed slaps, and a knee to the gut, she chokes Terry with her forearm until she struggles to breathe. Marcia presses her gun deep into her temple.

"How does it feel, huh? How does this feel? You think you're all big, bad and boujee, cause you own a cute lil' gun? I've been fuckin with guns since before you could even form sentences. You don't know shit about what's going on here and you have the nerve to…?!" Marcia chokes back tears.

"What's your name?"

Terry can't speak. All of her efforts are spent trying to wrestle Marcia to the ground, but Marcia is strong and firm. She's *unbelievably* strong with an unbreakable grip around her neck. Terry can barely move. She can hardly breathe, slapping and swatting about, hoping to make an impact, yet landing nothing. She gasps for air as burning tears stream from the corner of her bulging eyes.

"I said, what's your name," Marcia asks again as she loosens her hold just a bit.

Terry gasps for air swallowing way too much.

"Terry…" she screeches out, coughing violently and shaking with fear..

"Okay, Terry, do you have any children?"

"No," she gasps again. She begins to sink to the floor, but Marcia still holds a tight grip on her.

"Well, then you won't understand how it feels, when

the life is sucked out of you at the very thought that something has happened to your child. How you feel helpless when you can't reach them and you know that at any point in time, every second that you're not there to protect them, brings them closer and closer to the very danger you've tried to protect them from." Tears roll down Marcia's cheeks as Terry's face slowly begins to turn a slight shade of the color of her robe.

"Ruby is not like any other child, Terry! She's a part of him and this hell that he's created, whether she knows it or not. People have been plotting after him for years and because of his blood, she's his greatest weakness. The one thing that can bring down the man who holds all the power in this city…"

Terry collapses. Her hands fall to the floor, and then, she stops struggling. Marcia quickly releases her and Terry inhales the air she thought she'd never breathe again. Marcia stands above her, gun still drawn.

"Everyone wants power. Everyone wants the upper hand. But there's no room for everyone at the top. To his enemies, Cassius has no weakness. He cares about nothing. So, to defeat him seems impossible but everyone has a weakness, Terry. For Cassius, it's Ruby. *My* Ruby, and I refuse to let her near him."

Marcia collapses onto the floor beside her battered

opponent. She places her gun back inside of her purse and then stares quietly into Terry's eyes.

Unable to make sense of her near death experience, all Terry can do is stare back. She's looking at the mother of Cassius' child; sitting right there on the living room floor, right next to her.

"Look, Marcia, I- I'm sorry. I should never have drawn my weapon on you. I just didn't know who you were and...I'm so sorry."

Marcia blinks her tears away, but she wasn't ready for them to return with such force.

"Do you know where my...daughter...is?"

Terry, suddenly overwhelmed with empathy, now understands why Cassius never wanted to have children with her. She sees her future in Marcia and she's terrified. If Terry were to ever have kids with the man she loves, she can tell by Marcia's visit, her life would've been constant paranoia. She'd become overprotective, scared, defensive...crazy.

How can this woman live like this, she wonders? *I pulled a gun on her. All she wanted were answers and I was just another person standing in her way.*

She watches Marcia's face intently. It's dark and bold, yet there is an underlying vulnerability there. She barely knows the woman, but in her heart, she knows that if she were to ever go through what Marcia is going through, she'd never be able to survive it. This woman has suffered long and hard, but she's still strong. If only she could help her.

"I don't know where she is. I don't even know where Cassius is. He left the other night and never came back. He was upset that the person he sent to protect your daughter…"

Marcia looks away, afraid to hear what she would say next.

"…didn't want to be involved anymore. So, I think he thinks she's out there all alone…he may be trying to find her himself."

Marcia breaks down, letting out a long, hard scream as she cries.

"No, no, no… this can't be happening, not like this!" Marcia rocks back and forth,

Terry watches as Marcia heaves over in agony, embracing her knees for comfort. The tears well up once again.

"My baby's out there all alone. Oh God, please, no. Please."

Terry reaches over with a shaky hand to grab hold of Marcia's to comfort her. Marcia jumps from her touch.

"He has other people out there looking for her, Marcia, please, don't worry. Everything's gonna be ok."

"Terry, that's what I'm worried about! I feel in my heart that the people who are after her now, are the same people he sent out there to look for her!"

"Why...why would you say that?" Terry asks.

"Because when they tried to kill him last time, we were having dinner at our friend's house. No one followed us. They had to be there waiting for us outside, which means they knew we were coming. It had to be an inside job. No one outside of Cassius' close circle knew where my friend Patricia lived! It couldn't have been his rivals. They could never ever get that close to us. It had to be someone on the inside."

Terry listens but has no idea what Marcia is talking about, or who could have been behind this attempt to kill them all. She knows only one thing to do.

"Marcia, get up."

Marcia looks at her questioningly.

"I'm so sorry that you're going through all of this and there's not much that I can do, but I can take you to the place where Cassius goes when he needs a little guidance."

"Where...where are we going?"

"To the gym."

Chapter 9

Jerome turns off the Belt Parkway and onto the Van Wyck Expressway. It's six thirty. He's been in traffic all day. On the way to New York, he tried calling his wife to tell her that he'd spoken to Ruby, that he was on his way to get her, but she didn't pick up the phone—or maybe, she wouldn't. Her voicemail was full and she didn't return his texts. Either he had a poor signal on the highway or his wife was more furious with him than he'd thought. He tries to remain focused on getting his daughter home safely, without incident. His little feud with Marcia would have to wait.

Jerome pulls up to a house on 153rd Road and kills the engine. His stomach feels like a bubbling ocean of nerves.

One step in front of the other, Jerome.

He gets out and makes his way to the front door. This house has seen better days. The shutters could use a fresh coat of paint and the brick at the base of the structure is crumbling. He wonders if there are foundation issues. His concerns do nothing but prolong the task at hand. If he could have avoided this visit, he would have.

Jerome rings the doorbell five times and he waits impatiently. He notices a small scuff on the sole of his boot.

His wandering thoughts takes him on a distracting

journey from noticing the smallest amount of lint on his jacket to thoughts of retreat which grow stronger the longer he waits. Finally, the locks unlatch slowly from the other side. He brushes the lint from his clothes and straightens his posture. At the last second, he removes his hat and hides it behind his back.

Nana Brown peeks from behind the crack in the door, careful not to open it wider than a smidge. She isn't expecting anyone. She never expects anyone. No one *ever* comes to visit, besides a random church member bringing her and Pam a plate for Sunday dinner. But it isn't Sunday.

Her eyes widen.

"How dare you!" the words slither out of her mouth, breathy and slow.

Jerome stands before the old woman. Words escape him as his mouth refuses to comply.

"The nerve of you to show your face after all these years!"

The last time Jerome had seen her, she looked ten years younger. She very well may have been ten years younger. She had always been a sickly woman but back then, she had a little color to her cheeks. Now it looks as if all the blood has drained from her face. Her skin is dull, weathered, deeply creased and – pale. She's using a cane to support her weight, which can't be much because she's drowning in her house robes.

His throat tightens as he silently watches the frail old woman cling to life before his very eyes.

"Mrs. Brown, I really don't mean to intrude but, I wouldn't have come here unless it was an emergency. You see..."

Nana gasps. She tries to close the door on him with her all of her strength, but he's too strong. His foot is wedged in the door opening, preventing her from shutting him out completely. She continues to keep forcing the door closed on his foot, ignoring his cries.

"Mrs. Brown, please, please! I just want to come in for a second."

"NO!" she screams. "Get off of my porch right now!"

"Please, I just...I just need to know if you've seen Ruby. That's all. Have you seen my daughter, is she here?"

Nana grows quiet. The assault on Jerome and his foot cease. She allows him to enter. She inches backwards, breathing quickly, deeply. It was the most excitement she's had in years and at the mention of Ruby's name, all oxygen seemed to have escaped her. That name, Ruby, has been an omen in their household ever since her precious daughter Patricia was murdered. Ever since Nana found her bloody kitchen knife inside Pam's coat pocket, the night her granddaughter almost destroyed the house after meeting Ruby in the park, she hasn't been able to get a good night's rest.

"Look, I don't want any trouble, I really don't. I just haven't been able to find her and it's really important that I do. She could be in danger."

"What the hell is going on down there?" An angry voice echoes from the top of the stairs.

Jerome looks up to see a young woman about Ruby's age and she's a spitting image of her mother, Patricia.

Is she pregnant?

"I, um...stopped by to see if you've seen Ruby anywhere lately."

Pam, shocked to see Ruby's father in her house, descends very slowly.

What the hell is he doing here, she wonders. Her heart races as she recalls her last encounter with his daughter. It wasn't a pleasant one but there is no possible way that he would know about that, is there?

"Why would I have seen Ruby? What makes you think we know each other like that?!" Her face settles into a deep scowl as she scans him from head to toe.

Jerome swallows hard. Not the kind of attitude he'd expect from Patricia's daughter, but perhaps he can get a little more out of her if he treads carefully.

"I just assumed she was over here because she said that she was at a friend's house. I thought she meant you because we saw pictures from the wedding of both of you together and she's been out here in Queens for a while. We haven't been able to get in touch with her and I can't imagine her having any other friends out here but you."

Pam studies his face for a moment. She can't read him.

Does he know more than he's saying? Did Ruby call her parents and tell them about the incident in the park? Why is he really here?

"I'm sorry, but I don't know her like that and I haven't seen her."

Jerome stares back at her, standing at the bottom of the staircase.

Look at how her life has turned out, he thinks. *She doesn't deserve this.*

His thoughts are interrupted by Nana praying out loud. Unsure of what to do, he bows his head out of respect and waits for her to finish, but Pam is impatient.

"Nana, what are you ranting and raving about over there?" she asks. "You're always running your mouth, calling on Jesus. No wonder he ignores you. You don't know when to shut up!"

Jerome's lifts his head in shock. *What did she say?*

Nana looks at her poor, heartless granddaughter through misty eyes.

"What did you do, Pam?"

"Huh, what are you talking about now?" Pam asks nervously, glancing back and forth between her grandmother and Jerome.

"You know what I'm talkin' 'bout, girl!" Nana screeches.

"Look Nana, *you* don't know what you're talking about. Don't start with me today!" Pam descends the rest of the stairs, yelling in her grandmother's face. Jerome, unaware of the family dynamic, steps forward instinctively to protect the old woman. Pam is unhinged, deranged. She has to be, to talk to her Nana that way, a woman who has helped raise her since birth!

"Did you do something to that girl, Pam? Did you kill her?" Nana screams with every ounce of energy she has left. She stumbles backwards as Pam closes in on her. She begins to cough, each time harder than the last, and clutches her chest.

"Pam, back up, don't you see your grandmother is sick? And what's going on? Why is she asking if you killed Ruby?!"

Pam stands emotionless, facial expression – blank.

"She knows...she knows where she is, don't you? You hurt that poor girl, didn't you?" Nana says. She can't breathe well. She can hardly speak. She needs her oxygen mask but she can't get to it. Her chest continues to tighten and her arms and legs go numb. She continues to speak through shallow breaths, through the heartbreak.

"All these years I've taken care of you, I've tried to show you the right way. I took you to church and I been prayin' for you every day since I got you..." She takes another breath. "And you turned out so evil and...and nasty! You run away from home lookin' for whateva you was lookin' for out there in them streets...You left the church and now you're pregnant by that no-good boy! How could you do this? How could you hurt that girl like that!?"

Nana has to sit down. The pain in her chest is unbearable. She feels faint. Pam continues to stare at her with disgust, ignoring everything her grandmother said.

Jerome is trying to put the pieces together but something isn't making any sense.

Mrs. Brown asked if Pam killed my daughter! But why?

Jerome pushes past Pam and squats down next to Nana. He'd noticed that she'd been looking sicker the longer they'd been standing there. He isn't sure if she's this ill on a regular basis but he is becoming more worried about her health by the second.

"I said I didn't kill her!" Pam yells.

"But...but...you said..."

"I said I tried, I didn't say I actually did it!" Pam rolls her eyes. Although she sees her grandmother struggling to breathe, she shows no amount of empathy, not a bit.

"Please...Pa-, Pam...my...air..." Nana manages to get out. Jerome wipes the sweat off Nana's face.

"What...what is she talking about, her air?" He doesn't understand. Pam pretends not to notice Nana's eyes rolling into the back of her head.

"Oh, she's just talking about her oxygen mask," Pam waves her hand, dismissing the old woman.

"Well where is it?!" Jerome yells.

"In the living room," Pam responds nonchalantly. She doesn't make even the slightest movement to fetch it. Jerome runs into the living room with extreme urgency. He sifts through the junk cluttering the floor and sofas to locate it.

"Don't go running in there for that thing, she's fine. She only wants attention!" Pam yells after him. "Besides, she's like Lazarus. Just when you think 'that's it', she pops back up stronger than ever. She's immortal, that one there and unfortunately, I'm stuck with her forever."

He finally finds the green tank and mask set up in a corner of the room. He wheels it back to the foyer where Nana is slumped over on the floor. He sits her up and turns the tank on, adjusting the mask on her face and seeing that the oxygen is starting to do its job.

"What happened to you, Pam? How could you just sit there and watch your grandmother suffocate and not help her? Can't you see she's gravely ill? After all this woman has done for you? And what did you do to Ruby, where is she?" Jerome's voice is shaky, yet, firm.

Pam locks eyes with him. Her eyes are dark, wide and empty.

"After all that she's done for me? What has she done for me but be a pain all my life? *I've* had to take care of *her*! *I* worked *three* jobs to support us, I put food on the table cause her disability ain't shit! I bust my behind all day every day just to live in this ugly-ass-ratchet-ass-rickety-ass house! She ain't do nothing for me but make my life a living hell!"

Jerome is stunned into silence. Nana tries to catch her breath as tears creep from beneath the mask.

"And you want to know why I tried to kill Ruby? It's because I hate her. I hate her so much, it's all I think about! Answer me this. How is it that *that* girl has everything I could only dream of, yet, here we all are and as you can see, I have absolutely nothing? We were both there in that house fifteen years ago. The both of us! The only difference between us is, I lost my mother! She didn't! Her's got to kiss her good night, her's took her to school, and I bet she went to the *best* ones. She's got expensive shit, too! I saw that ride of hers. Real nice. And I bet ya'll live in a nice, big, happy clean home, right? You know who I had to live with? Nana and a whole family of roaches and rats! And we barely had enough food to eat.

She steps to him, inches from his face.

"Do you know what it's like to go to bed hungry, Jerome? To have to get up early to stand in line for the soup kitchen? Bagging groceries to make pennies? Being laughed at for wearing dirty clothes to school because we couldn't afford the wash? How is it that *that* girl got everything and kept her mother too, when I lost mine and was left with nothing?"

Hot tears scorch her face. Jerome lowers his head in shame.

"We tried," he slowly whispers.

Pam stops sniffling.

"What do you mean, 'We tried'?"

"We tried to help you and your grandmother, Pam. We

tried to send you money…we tried to move you elsewhere but your grandmother would have none of it." Jerome wipes his eyes as he continues. "Every check we sent came right back and she didn't want us to see you or have anything to do with you. She wanted to take care of you and that was it."

Pam glares down at her grandmother.

"You did *what*?!" she yells.

"It was for your own good, chil'. I didn't want *no* blood money or *no* drug money comin' up in my house for you. That's how ya momma got killed, messin' around with that stuff and I…I…didn't want the…same thing…for you."

Nana takes a staggered deep breath, "The devil already took my baby…I wasn't gonna let him take my grandbaby too," she manages to say.

Pam glares at Jerome. She shakes her head as she tries to make sense of everything she'd just heard. Nana starts to shake a little. She complains about piercing pains in her chest, neck, and back. Jerome stares at her, panicked.

"She's having a heart attack! Call 911, Pam, hurry!"

"How do you know all of this…I don't even know you like that…did Marcia tell you everything?"

"Pam, this is not the time. I need you to call for an ambulance!"

"Not until you answer my question!"

"I can't believe what I'm hearing! Your grandmother is literally dying on the floor right in front of you and you could care less? You are *nothing* like your mother!"

"What do you know about my mother? Why do you even care?!"

"Because," he says as he dials the police from his own phone, "I had to...you're my daughter."

Chapter 10

Sean gets off the bus in Astoria, Queens. The wind blows intensely, drying his eyes quicker than it takes for them to tear. He walks down a familiar block with his head lowered, half of his face buried beneath the collar of his coat. The air grows colder the longer the day wanes on.

With every whipping gust, Sean wishes he'd taken his car after all. He'd left it at David's house for fear that he'd be followed. There's only one place he can go is where no one will ever look for him.

"Hey Pablo, let me get a mild and a book of matches," he says.

"Sure, papi." The cashier at a well-lit bodega hands over the cigars while trying to get a better look at the face beneath the hood.

"Sean?"

Sean looks up slowly. He knew he should've kept walking.

"Mirar, what the wind blew in! Sean! Where have you been, man? I haven't seen you since you were un niño," says Pablo, his hands hovering at the level of his nose. "Talk about a blast from the past!"

"I've been around, workin', you know?" Sean replies

as he keeps an eye on the door. It had been some time since he'd seen Pablo but now is not the time to talk. He's sure he'd taken every winding train and bus route to get there, but he can't be too sure he wasn't followed.

Pablo's eyes shine bright, they're older and tired, but he's excited to see him. Sean can't just brush him off like that. The man used to give him free cold cuts to snack on and put slabs of steak on his bruises when he got into fights with the kids from around the block. He'd watched out for him too many times to count and he definitely took care of him when he was hungry. Pablo gave him his first job as a delivery boy. Sean could never forget that.

"Si, workin' is all we do, huh? Never get time to live, hijo." Pablo's smile begins to fade.

"How's that mother of yours?"

"I wouldn't know...we don't talk," Sean replies.

"I don't blame you. But didn't you stop this smoking stuff? I told you it was bad for you."

"I know, I haven't smoked in years, but I need one right now to take the edge off."

"I'm sorry to hear that," says Pablo as he rings him up. "Don't let this become a habit again, hijo. You take care of yourself and come by again soon." He hands Sean his purchase and with a quick nod, Pablo watches him brave the cold and disappear into the wind that blew in with him.

Sean takes a seat on a park bench about a hundred feet away from Pablo's store. As he champs his mild, he frequently stops to blow warm air into his hands to keep them from freezing. It's the beginning of April but it's so cold, it feels like winter! The sky is dark gray, the trees are still bare and the wind doesn't seem to be letting up.

He lights his cigar and takes a long drag, indulging in the moment, a moment he never thought he'd experience again. As the smoke fills his lungs, he holds it in for as long as he can, void of oxygen, allowing the vignette of darkness to swirl around his vision and then, at the last second before he loses consciousness, he exhales, watching the curls of white smoke blend with the stream of steam escaping from his mouth.

He surveys the area while he smokes. There's no one here but him. A few garbage cans overflowing and the usual crackheads sitting at a table shooting venom into their veins. The swings are the same broken swings as when he was a kid and the park seemed to have lost the life it once had. It looked the same back then; broken, run down and neglected, but as a child he and his friends were able to make the best of what they had. This broken, run-down park was a fortress, a space center, an undiscovered planet, but it took a lot of imagination. Kids nowadays don't have any. They'd rather stay inside on cold windy days like this and zombie out on their phones and tablets. For Sean, there was freedom in imagination and this park was the one place where he could think. But his life is starting to look eerily similar to this park. His imagination may not be strong enough for him to see past the destruction to better days ahead.

Sean watches the female addict prance around the table, unable to sit still. She hovers over her man and after he swats her away a few times, she goes back to prancing around the table and scratching herself. She repeats this over and over again until her partner lets her sit down to receive her hit. The man pulls a white rock out of his pocket and places it onto a spoon, flicking a lighter that refuses to produce a spark. He glances over at Sean.

"Aye, man, you got a light?"

Sean slowly blows the smoke from his mouth and turns away. The addicts, growing desperate to get their hit, are back to trying to produce a spark again.

Sean is disgusted at their worthlessness; empty humans without substance, no purpose in life. All they do is take up space. They're festering sores on the face of the community he had grown to love and until recently, had grown to hate.

He fingers the book of matches in his pocket he'd just bought from Pablo. He'd be damned if he was going to help them kill themselves. He scans the park again. He's still alone. No one had followed him. There's no one there but him. The junkies at the table aren't people, just empty shells of who they used to be.

Suddenly, kids run out of Pablo's store, some carrying a small paper bag, probably filled with candy or Hostess snacks, and others carrying plastic shopping bags more than likely filled with items from a grocery list. He smiles as two boys drop their grocery bags filled with food and race to the end of the street. A little girl, about seven, trails behind them struggling with both bags and yelling after them about how she's gonna tell Momma they was playin' around again instead of going straight home like she said. The children continue to play and a warm spot grows within his chest. Perhaps there's still some imagination left in this little pocket of hell he used to call home.

"Aye, c'mon man, I see you smokin'. You ain't got no light?

"No, I don't have no light for you, man! Get out of my face." Sean takes another long drag and turns the other way.

"C'mon, me and my woman can't get right unless we

have a light man. Come on… Please?"

Sean refuses to acknowledge him any further.

"Aight, look, look…for a light, my woman will suck your…" This grabs Sean's attention but not for the reasons the man had hoped.

"Okay, I can see you don't like that. How 'bout I…"

"Get the hell out of my face and don't ever come back around here again or I swear to god…" Sean fiddles with something in his pocket and the couple flees, afraid of what it might be. The blood boils beneath his skin. Disgusting…shooting up right across the street from kids…and in a park, no less? *What happened to my neighborhood?*

He tries to relax. He takes a few more hits of his cigar, feeling the tobacco course through his lungs and relaxing him the way he'd hoped it would.

The stress is overwhelming. He has to control it somehow. Picking up an old smoking habit seemed to be the best solution at the moment. But the more he smokes, the more he remembers why he quit in the first place.

How am I ever going to get over all of this crap with Ruby? I left her in the middle of the night after making love to her for the first time. After weeks of leading up to it, I just leave her like that?

He slams his fist, hard on the park bench.

I lied to her. I don't love Pam, I don't want anything to do with that crazy slut. But I knew it would devastate her. It was the only way I could make sure she wouldn't have anything else to do with me. Wasn't it? I had no choice, right?

Sean is heartbroken as he retraces his steps over the past few weeks, leading up to this moment, here in this run-down park. One thing is for certain, he loves her, more than anything he has ever felt in his entire life. She brings him life, gives him something to work towards, to love for. If It weren't for this situation with Scully and her connection to him, he would never have abandoned her. The thought of abandoning her sits in his stomach like a ton of bricks. That is what he did to her. There's no way around it, no words to ease the gravity of his betrayal. He abandoned the woman he loves, because he is a coward. Rather than be honest and tell her the truth, he'd rather break her heart. Some man he is.

The truth. That's another problem in itself. After leaving Ruby, Sean had had enough. He called Scully to resign and there was nothing that Scully could do or say to change his mind, not even the threat of death. He wanted out. It sickened him to see the pictures from Sheila's and Ruby's file back at David's house with a younger Scully, front and center, talking with the police. Everything had all of a sudden become so complicated and he couldn't be involved any longer.

Now, he sits on a park bench with nothing to do. Nowhere to go. He can't go back to his apartment because the people who want him dead will probably look for him there. Going to the gym is out of the question. After listening to Scully threaten to kill him in every way possible, he knew that running into him was a death wish. He truly has no place to go in a city run by a ruthless drug lord and furious father.

Now is time for survival, he thinks to himself. He needs a plan. He quit his job as bookkeeper so early he hadn't enough money saved up to leave town. He knows better than to approach his old idiot supervisor back at the warehouse to ask for his job back because the man couldn't wait to get rid of him anyway. He remembered rumors from his coworkers that if you were in a bad spot, the owner, who always remained anonymous, would give you a loan to get you back on your feet. But Sean can't in good conscience put himself in the position to be at the will of someone else more powerful than him. He needs to be in control of his situation and right now, he's running low on options.

So here he is, jobless, hopeless, and homeless. He rubs his scalp; he's worse off than when he started. What is he going to do now?

To his right, a few houses down, is the home he'd grown up in. He walks towards it, breathing in cold air, deeply. Maybe someone is home; hopefully his mother won't turn him away.

Sean knocks on the door twice and waits for an answer. He wraps his arms tightly around his body to keep warm. He's having second thoughts about being there, but he has nowhere else to go. He hadn't spoken to his mother in months and even when they were speaking, he couldn't stand to be in her presence.

Desperate times, desperate measures. He'd been traveling all night, transferring from buses to trains, trying to figure out where he should go next. He walked around aimlessly until his travels brought him to this familiar place. No one would look for him here. This is the last place on earth he would ever be.

The door finally opens. His brother Damian, who stands at just about the same height as Scan, holds the door open wide. Neither of them move a muscle. They both share similar features that they inherited from their mother but it's clear, they didn't share the same father. Their mother's skin is a deep chocolate brown and while Sean's is a milky cinnamon complexion, Damian's shade is that of a dark berry. Damian's skin glistens although it isn't oily, and his lips are much fuller, a deeper red than Sean's. His features are chiseled to perfection and Damian is well aware of his attractiveness. He wears it like a suit.

Sean meets him eye to eye. The last time they'd seen each other, Sean was chasing him out of his house after he walked in on him six-inches deep inside of Pam. Damian seemed to take a little caution by standing back from the door, putting about five feet of space between them. He nervously smiles.

"Hey, Sean...long time no see, man. You comin' in?" Damian asks nervously.

Sean slowly enters the house as Damian inches his way backwards, still trying to retain the distance. Sean stands in the center of the room. The house, is still the same. They had the same old furniture with the plastic coverings, a dirty table full of old newspapers and unopened mail, and the carpet was the same rust-colored shag carpet that it had always been.

Nothing much has changed here except for the walls. He notices the empty spaces where his pictures used to hang and it twists at his gut. He never used to have as many as his younger brother but still, they were up there—at least they used to be. He continues to glance around the room and eventually walks over to the piano where his mother kept pictures from their childhood and mementos they'd collected.

His heart sinks when he picks up a frame that used to hold a picture of him and his brother, smiling and holding hands, proud of the snowman they'd just built. But now it's just a picture of Damian, smiling at the lone snowman. It's obvious his mother cut him out. It's even more obvious that she'd cut him out of their entire lives by removing everything that bore his image.

The pain is unbearable and as he places the picture back down on the piano, he turns to Damian. He stands there in total silence watching in misery as his older brother discovers just how much their mother truly hates him.

He was never for any of this, Damian thinks. He'd made an unforgivable mistake with what he had done to Sean, and his mother couldn't care less. She always cared more for him than she did for Sean, which only made their relationship more distant.

If Pam hadn't gotten him so drunk that night, he probably would never have gone through with it. He'd always had a slight crush on her, but he'd never acted on it before. Something was off that night he met up with her at his brother's house. She caught him on a night when his guard was down and he'd regretted it ever since.

But he can barely remember that night. If it weren't for Sean filling him in while he was wailing on him, he wouldn't have remembered a thing. The next morning when he'd awakened at home, his head was throbbing. He'd never blacked out drunk like that before. What did she give him? His mother screamed at the dried blood and cuts on his beautiful face. No matter what he told his mother about what he *could* remember, she blamed Sean for everything.

His mother had no sympathy for her oldest son. She didn't like Pam to begin with but she hated Sean even more. So, when he came home looking for his brother, his mother jumped to Damian's defense and cursed him to hell. Damian couldn't stop it, even if he wanted to. He was more afraid of her than anyone even Sean. Her tongue spit hellfire when she spoke, and her words cut deep into the spirit. Damian didn't know what he would do if she ever treated him the way she treated his brother. How any man could remain one after a lashing like that, is admirable.

Sean's eyes become redder and wetter by the second. The pain is contagious. Damian thrusts his hands towards his face and wipes away the moistness from his eyes before his brother notices.

"I shouldn't be here." Sean takes a deep breath and swallows hard. "This was a mistake."

Sean walks towards the door, stepping out of the way just seconds before it bursts open with his mother, struggling through the doorway lugging overflowing bags of groceries. She stumbles as one of the bags falls to the floor with a jar of tomato sauce breaking into pieces and splattering all over her freshly mopped kitchen tile.

"Ugh!" she screams. "Dame, come get this up for me!" she yells into the house. She's so busy trying to get organized, she doesn't even notice Damian is already standing right in front of her, and so is Sean.

"DAMIAN!" She yells again.

"Ma, I'm right here," he says.

"Well why you didn't answer me the first..."

How could she not have seen him when she came in? How could she not have seen her oldest son right in front of her face? She straightens and silently gathers herself, the groceries in her arms frozen in place. No one moves until Damian takes a step forward to clean up the mess like his mother had told him.

"No, don't you move, Damian. What is he doing in my house?" Damian's head is down and he glances at Sean out of the corner of his eyes to see if he would speak up for him.

"I SAID, what is he *doing* in my *house*, Damian?"

"Um, I don't know...he...he just got here." Their mother turns back to Sean and raises her eyebrow. He understands what she means. She wants to know the answer and someone had better tell her quick.

"I was, um, in the ah…neighborhood, and I just stopped by to say hello but-"

"…But what? You think you're welcome here, you think you can just pop up whenever you feel like it?"

"No," Sean is trying to calm down but his emotions rage inside of him.

"So, I don't understand why you're here. You know I don't want you in my house! You are no son of mine and I don't care to ever see you again. Did I make myself clear?"

"Crystal," he replies through gritted teeth. He walks towards the door but Damian grabs his arm.

"You don't have to leave, Sean. This is your home too."

Their mother stops placing the bags of food on the counter and glares at her youngest son.

"And who the *hell* do you think you are, telling him that he can stay here? This is *my* house!" She continues to scream at the top of her lungs, saying anything and everything that comes to mind. She paces around the kitchen, slamming cabinets as she puts the food away, telling Sean she regretted giving birth to him.

Damian cleans up around Sean as he stands there planted to the ground. He can't move. It's like he's in a trance.

Her words just seep in, making him wish for death. He tries to open his mouth to speak but it's as if he's having an out-of-body experience. He hears himself saying something but he can't comprehend what it is. It sounds like a bunch of noise but that doesn't stop him from trying harder. He stares at the ground and finally finds his voice.

"Why do you hate me so much?"

Damian stops mopping and their mother stops screaming.

"What?"

"I said, why do you hate me so much?"

"You don't even understand," she rolls her eyes and goes back to what she was doing.

"So then tell him, mom! Tell him!" Damian yells. He's so fed up, he can't take her abuse towards his brother any longer. She's shocked. Damian has *never* had the nerve to talk to her like that and what's worse, he seems to be standing up for his brother.

"You want to know, you really want to know?" She slams the fridge shut and meets Sean face to face.

"I had you so young; I had to give up *everything* in life...my dreams, my social life, and my family.

"They disowned me because I was seventeen with a baby. I struggled and couldn't keep a steady job because I had to bring you everywhere with me. You were *such* a burden, it was unreal. You cried and cried, my friends spoiled you and you needed everything all the time. I had nothing for myself! Everything was about you! The baby needs food, the baby needs diapers, the baby needs this, needs that…Oh my God! I wanted to go to college, I wanted to model and sing. The world was calling me," she continues reminiscing with a half smile on her face, "and I thought I was in love. I was in love with a dream that would never come true and a man who loved everything but me. He had other women, other children, spent money on dumb stuff but couldn't give me a dime to take care of you! He told me he loved me, took me out a few times but that was it! He couldn't care less that he had a son. He was all about the streets, the drugs, the women, and the money and I couldn't stand it."

Sean's heart breaks even more with every word that flies out of her mouth, blaming him for her misfortunes. He keeps it in, not wanting to let her see that she is hurting him, but it's tough.

She's never spoken of his father before. From what she's telling him now, his father's characteristics are very similar to a man he'd recently embraced as a father figure.

"All of these years, I've struggled to make the mortgage, to put food on the table and clothes on your back. If

I went to college, I'd have a degree and I'd have more money, a better place, and a better life, and the reason why I don't have it is because of you. You and your father look just alike, and *that* is the reason why I *hate* you, now get out!"

His life. This is his life. Weeks ago, he thought he was at his low point, but, now he's certain that *this* is his lowest. His mind wanders. He finds himself thinking about his imaginary father. His father couldn't be Scully, could it? They're all from the same hood, and from what he's gathered from the stories from Scully and from Sheila's and Ruby's file, the timing matches up. He's afraid to ask. If he thought his mother hated him now just for being the son of a man she hates the most, he can imagine how much more she could despise him if she finds out that he is hanging out with a kingpin. He can't bear the thought of being in love with his half-sister. It's impossible. He loves her too much. Could this be true, could he really be in love with his own sister?

He shakes the disturbing thoughts out of his head. He's getting way too far ahead of himself. He doesn't know if Scully is his father or not, but he did say that he looked at him like a son.

Does he know something that I don't?

Sean contemplates the possibilities of him being Scully's unclaimed son. The odds are frighteningly high.

As he thinks about it, he can't help but think of Ruby. Maybe he needs to go back and make things right with her after all. It's obvious that he isn't wanted anywhere around here and if Ruby feels anything close to how he felt when his mother admitted that she didn't love him, he urgently needs to go back to her and rectify his mistake.

"Didn't you hear what I said? Get the hell out of my house!"

As Sean makes his way towards the door, Damian pulls him into a bear hug and cries on his brother's shoulder.

"Sean, I am so sorry about what I did. I regret it every day and I can't live with myself for hurting you like that. I love you so much and no matter what she says, you're not who she says you are! You're still my brother and I love you."

Sean let go of his younger brother, smiling as his eyes wells up with tears.

"I love you too."

Sean turns to leave but the door flies open just as it did earlier when his mother arrived. This time, a familiar face walks through the door. It's Trisha, Ruby's cousin, carrying her youngest child.

"Damian, can you go get the baby bag out of the car?" she asks as she tries to balance the baby, a car seat, and her purse.

"Sean, what are you doing here?" Everyone looks at each other, confused and shocked.

"Trisha, this is my brother Sean. You know him?" asks Damian.

"Do I know him? Of course, I know him, he's talkin' to my cousin Ruby. Wait...you have a brother?" Trisha asks, completely confused.

"Trisha, what are you doing here?" Sean asks.

"Damian is the father of my youngest baby. I always come over here." Sean looks at the baby and then his brother.

"I thought you were dating Pam, Dame?" Sean blurts out right before Damian could stop him from saying anything.

"Pam...PAM...that slut Pam that's messing with my cousin? Are you serious? That's that chick that be callin' at all hours of the night?" she screams. "How long you been seein' her, huh Damian, HUH? You was at the club with her not too long ago right...'cause my cousin Ruby told me she saw Pam there with somebody named Damian and described you to a tee!"

"Trish.., look...it's not like that...I... I mean we went out but-"

"See, that's that bull! She said you had a job and was in school and that's what threw me off...so you lyin' about that too?"

167

"I do have a job and I do go to school, Trish...I just didn't tell you 'cause..."

"My baby needs milk and you got a freaking job and you ain't tell me...what else didn't you tell me?"

Sean shakes his head as he watches his brother desperately try to explain his relationship with Pam to his baby's mother. His own mother storms out of the kitchen towards them all.

"Get out, Sean! You see what you started up in here? Nothing good ever comes when you're here. Now get out!"

As Sean walks down the driveway he continues to hear Trisha screaming at Damian.

"What you mean, you got her pregnant?!"

Chapter 11

It's a bumpy ride to nowhere as a New York City MTA bus manages to hit every bump, pothole, and crack in the road. After every stop, the bus accelerates abruptly, pushing Ruby backwards into her seat while letting off enough fumes to impact the ozone all on its own. The loud humming of the engine and squealing brakes is deafening, but no one else seems to mind. Watching the other passengers is like watching a cluster of androids on autopilot. One second, their faces are buried in their phones and the next, they're on their feet, waiting to exit the bus, never once altering their line of vision.

It's impressive. Ruby watches a young mother of three small children balance a baby on her hip and tend to the other two who are swinging from pole to pole. These children had full control of their limbs on the bumpy bus, never once falling into anyone else. Ruby wasn't as lucky when she first boarded. As soon as the bus pulled away from the curb, she clumsily grabbed for the handles above the seats and missed, stumbling into an old woman who, luckily, was kind and very forgiving.

She'd apologized and tried to explain that it was her first time riding public transportation, and she vaguely remembers the woman saying something about getting her "bus legs," which are apparently very different from "train legs." Ruby smiled kindly and proceeded to find an open seat. She was in no mood to talk. Her life is in turmoil. She just needs a moment to think, a moment to breathe.

Until this moment she hadn't had time to herself to really consider who she is and what it is that she wants to get out of this whole ordeal. Of course she wants to prove her mother innocent, should Pam follow through on her word to report her mother to the authorities, but there's something more. There is something more that she needs to get to the bottom of and it's a question she's been asking her entire life.

What is everyone hiding from me? she ponders. *Why must I go through* all of this *to find the truth about my past, about my mother, about...Pam? Clearly Pam is psycho but she didn't get that way overnight. What really happened to her? What causes a person to want to kill someone? To want to kill me? And Sean?*

It can't be Sean, can it? I mean, she was deeply in love with him, so I understand her hating my guts right now, but she had a game plan to meet me at my mother's wedding before Sean was even on my radar. That girl has hated me her entire life.

And my parents, forget it! They never even mentioned

Pam or her mother's death to me. Why?

Speaking of my parents, Sheila and David are acting just like them. Telling me to talk to Sean about something important, but, why the hell can't she *tell me? What does he have to do with anything? I mean Sheila and I are in this together, aren't we? Well, we were until David came along. She's been acting really odd. It's almost like she has more information and refuses to share it with me. Why?!*

Why does no one trust me? What have I done to lose the trust of the ones I love? It makes no sense. Sheila's getting secret text messages, but I'm *the one who can't be trusted?*

A migraine settles in and her temples throb from the endless contemplation over her life. Ruby attempts to relieve the pain by applying pressure but it's no use. The stress has finally begun to settle in and it doesn't seem as if it will be letting up any time soon.

The bus comes to a stop on the side of the road to load and unload another group of passengers and Ruby notices a young man embracing his partner, not yet ready to say goodbye. Thoughts of Sean begin to overshadow all forms of critical thinking and self-pity.

How could he...how could he just leave *me like that? It's so unlike him. Or is it? I don't know him as well as I thought I did.* The bus pulls off again and as the city flies by, she blankly stares out the window.

I thought we were getting somewhere. I finally gave in, I allowed myself to fall in love with him and...he said he loved me too. The way he said it, the way he touched me, that was real. It had to be!"

She reminisces over every whisper, the touch of his fingers, where his lips left a trail of invisible kisses. The memory is too painful.

It just doesn't make any sense. He's wanted to be with me since the moment we met, and once I spend one night with him, he's out? How could he choose Pam over me? That crazy, murderous-plotting, psychotic ...!

Anger rises from the pit of her belly; her eyes red hot with tears. She can't find her way through her emotions. She's devoid of solutions and the weight of her feud with her parents, her fight with Sheila, and now, Sean abandoning her for Pam...it's too much to bear.

She can't breathe. She needs off of this bus, now. But as she begins to stand, she realizes the bus is still moving. She'll have to wait for the next stop.

She rests her head on the window and looks out at the cold city again, wondering how long this anxiety will last. She has no idea where she's going, no idea what she is going to do next, but as soon as the thought of giving up and running back home to her mommy enters her mind, the overwhelming power of love she has for her mother jolts her back to life, reminding her of her purpose, of her mission.

I came all this way to find Pam's mother's murderer. My mother may get on my nerves at times and drive me crazy, but no one is going to take my mother from me. Not even Pam. She wants me to feel the pain she felt growing up without one, but I refuse to let her win. I will prove my mother innocent and uncover the truth everyone's been keeping from me. I'm nearly there! I can feel it!*

If she's going to figure out the rest of this on her own, she definitely needs her car, but the problem is, she has no idea how to get there. Nothing on this bus route looks familiar, at all.

The bus stops again but Ruby decides to stay on. The area is rough and doesn't look like the safest place to ask for directions. Someone had just made the bus before the driver closed its doors.

He swipes his Metro card and hurriedly makes his way to the back of the bus, finding an empty seat five seats away from Ruby. He catches his breath and smiles at her.

"Almost missed it," he chuckles as he adjusts his fitted cap and sweatshirt. Ruby barely smiles and quickly turns the other way. Since he boarded, she'd noticed him watching her on more than one occasion. Beginning to feel uncomfortable, she tries to focus straight ahead and she sees the same old lady that she'd fallen on earlier, watching her as well.

What are they staring at, she wonders? Does she have something on her face? She quickly swipes the back of her hand over her mouth and eyes, just in case. But the man in the sweatshirt and the old woman continue to glance at her every so often.

Ruby begins to say something to the man behind her when she feels a slight tap on her thigh. She turns around to face the old woman, who had gotten up to move closer to her. Now that they're face to face, the woman reminds her of her Granny, Jerome's mother.

The woman is wrapped in a long, camel-colored pea coat, with a multicolored knitted scarf and cap. No wonder she reminds her of Granny. They both have an affinity for knit wear. As the woman smiles, her pearly white dentures glisten behind her thin lips and the lines in her face deepen.

"Are you that young lady from that wedding?" The woman asks quietly.

"Wedding?"

"Yes, honey, the wedding that took place a few weeks ago here in Queens. It was like a big Cinderella ball and all of those important people were there, and photographers and

174

limos…"

"Oh," Ruby remembers. The wedding felt like ages ago. So much had happened since then. "Yes, I was there, but, how did you know that?"

"You folks were in the paper for a couple of days. It was magical! That wedding was the biggest thing out here anyone has seen in a long time."

Ruby glances around again and catches the eyes of a few people looking her way. An elderly couple coyly smiles at her. She waves back, respectfully, and their smiles grow wider, happy to have been acknowledged at all.

"Is that why people keep looking at me?" she asks.

"Probably," the woman laughs. "You and your family were like local celebrities out here in our neighborhood. It was such a *spectacular* event, me and my granddaughters watched it from the TV and all they kept saying was how beautiful you and your mother were and how your dress was so pretty." She chuckles again. "They want to get a dress made like yours for their prom."

Ruby is grateful to have someone to distract her from her troubling thoughts.

"That is so sweet. I know a great dress maker…"

The woman laughs again and pats Ruby on her knee. "Oh no, they're only six and five. They have a long way to go before they go to any prom, honey."

Ruby and the little woman laugh together and for the first time in a while, it felt good to finally talk to someone other than Sheila, Sean, or her parents. She'd been so caught up and focused on her own life, she hadn't realized until now that life was still going on around her. Even the little things made a difference in other people's lives, whether she knew it or not, and her parents' wedding brought joy to a neighborhood she barely knew.

"What are you doing taking the bus, girl? You shouldn't be out here alone." The woman chastised. "Don't you have a vehicle?"

"Yes, I do but it's on Sutton Avenue and I'm trying to get to it. Do you know which bus takes me there? I've been on this one for over an hour and I think I'm lost."

The woman tells her how to get there from the next stop but her voice begins to fade.

"What...did I say something wrong?" Ruby asks.

"No," she whispers. She leaned in closer to Ruby and speaks quietly.

"You watch out for that one," she says nodding her head towards the man in the sweatshirt. "I've been watching him ever since he came on this bus and he been starin' at you more than anyone in here. I watched him out the window when we got to his stop and he looked like he had no intentions on catching this bus 'til he saw you."

Ruby glances in his direction again and see's that he's on the phone. She can't make out what he's saying and it's probably because he's speaking so quietly.

"Are you sure?" Ruby asks with uncertainty, but the woman pays her no mind.

"Honey, look at me. I've been around a long time, I know if something's wrong when I see it." She looks deep into Ruby's eyes. "Do you have anything on you...to protect yourself?"

"Um, no, not really," Ruby admits. The woman opens her large purse and takes out a can of pepper spray and hands it to her.

"I can't take this...this is yours. What if you need it?"

The lady chuckles again.

"Chal, look how old I am. Ain't nobody doin' nothing to me, besides I had that thing for years and ain't never used it once.

"See, so I probably won't need to use it either since you never did," Ruby says, still pleading with the woman to take it back. The woman's eyes soften as she leans in to pinch Ruby's cheeks.

"I ain't never been as pretty as you, either." She pats

Ruby's face, making her young new friend smile at the unexpected yet, much needed compliment. Since Sean left her this morning, she'd never felt so insecure, but this little lady was heaven sent.

The bus slows down to a complete stop.

"Now get up before you miss your stop and remember what I told you." She winks as Ruby grabs her purse and scurries down the aisle. She relishes the thought of telling her grandbabies who she'd run into on the bus today. As she watches Ruby leave the bus and head in the right direction, she waves goodbye to her young friend, silently praying to God to keep her safe and to watch over her as she travels home.

The woman is relieved when the bus finally pulls off with the man she'd been watching still in his seat and on the phone, but the relief is short-lived. He jumps to his feet and runs to the front of the bus and demands to be let off immediately.

The bus stops again and the man is let off. As it pulls off again, the elderly woman turns around in her seat and peers out of the window behind her. The man who'd been eyeing that sweet young lady walked in the same direction as she did. As he reaches the sidewalk, she watches him pull up his black hood and smile at her as the bus pulls away.

Chapter 12

Sheila quickly jumps out of the shower and gets dressed, preparing to meet Mike at a coffee shop in Manhattan. He has a lot of explaining to do and she can't wait to hear it. After what happened last night and after Sean's unexpected confession, she has to be getting closer to finding out who is responsible for killing Pam's mother and her father, and who is trying to kill Ruby.

"David, I'm about to leave," she shouts up the stairs. "Tell Ruby I'll come with y'all when y'all head back to Jersey."

"Sheila, wait!" he yells from the back room. "Ruby's not up here!"

"What?" she drops her purse onto the couch and runs up the stairs to find David standing in the room Ruby slept in the night before.

"She's gone," he says, "I knocked on the door to ask her if she was ok but when I came in after she didn't answer, there was a note on her bed."

"A note?! What is she? A serial killer? Why didn't she just text us?"

David rolls his eyes.

179

"Maybe she didn't want us to know right away Sheila, c'mon. You're smarter than that. You're letting your emotions cloud your judgment."

"Well, what does it say, David?! And why are you tutoring me when Ruby is missing?" Sheila yells. The oxygen in the room seems to be getting thinner the longer it takes for David to read the note.

Her skin crawls at the thought of Ruby being out there alone on the streets of New York, especially now that she's truly aware of the danger that awaits her little cousin should it find her.

"I'll read it to you," David offers.

"Sheila, I can't thank you enough for being there and coming this far with me. It's been a tough journey and I couldn't have done it without you. This unfortunate issue has brought us closer than we've ever been, but I also feel it is beginning to tear us apart. There are certain things I just don't understand, and in order to, I need to be on my own. This is my journey, my issue and my problem. I feel myself changing, becoming more skeptical and untrusting, even more so lately.

I can't go on knowing that this could potentially change you too. You have a higher calling and this…this is just a horrible distraction. I can carry my own burden from here on out. Thank you for your love and support. I'll keep in touch, but please, don't come looking for me. I need to do this on my own.

With Love,

Ruby

"That girl is crazy!" Sheila says, snatching the paper out of David's hand and re-reading it as if she didn't believe him. "What kind of passive aggressive BS is this? A distraction for *me*? I live for this! I breathe this, I *study* this, David! Who the hell does she think she's talking to? She's the one who doesn't know a damn thing about…about…anything! She's got some nerve!"

"I know, but do you have any idea where she could have gone," asks David. He paces around the room rubbing the back of his neck.

"Maybe she went back to my house?" Sheila assumes.

"You think so? She has to be smarter than that. Why would she go back there when she knows those guys will probably have that place scoped?"

"Because," she says, "Ruby's not built for these streets. If she's riding public transportation now, she won't be for long 'cause that's too crazy for her. She wasn't raised like that, so she'll need something familiar to her…her car."

"All right, so what do you want to do? Don't you have to meet Mike soon?"

"Yeah, I do, and as much as I want to see her and ring her *freaking* neck, I have to go to Mike and hear what he has to tell me. I believe he's gonna bust this case wide open and the quicker I find out, the quicker we can solve this and Ruby will be safe. Do you mind going over to the house to see if she's there?"

"Sure. Hopefully, she'll be the only one there."

*****

Sheila walks into the Starbucks located on Broadway and Barclay and takes a seat in the furthest corner of the store, far away from everyone else. She's early but still, she waits impatiently. Mike enters a few minutes later and takes a seat.

"Hey."

"Hey."

"You want anything…coffee, Danish, a latte?" he asks.

"No, Mike. I want to know what's going on."

Mike takes a deep breath, looking around the room before speaking.

"Ok, where do I start?"

"How about from the beginning," she offers, still impatient.

"Aight, so I worked for this white guy for a while sellin' weed and remember that day I was supposed to meet you and Rube at the club, but I never came?"

"Yeah…" Sheila blinks sarcastically as she remembers how much of her time he wasted that night.

"Well, I was at his house and he pretty much gave me the full rundown of what he actually does and that he's been training me without me knowing it. I definitely wanted to make way more money than what I was making and he told me how. He gave me a ton of cash to get me started; to get my house and my whip and he broke down how the system works," he says.

"How does it work?" Sheila asks, leaning closer. This is what she's been waiting for.

"Basically, it's a franchise and there is one main boss. Under this one boss, the five boroughs are divided up among five men called Pieces."

"What's a Piece?" she asks, confused about the title.

"Sheila look, you're gonna have to keep up 'cause I can't keep repeating myself. The five men are called Pieces."

"I know that, but why are they *called* that?"

"Just think about chess. You know how to play chess?"

"Yeah, a li'l bit."

"Ok. This whole thing is like a big game of chess. If you understand how chess works, you understand how this works. Think of the big boss as the main player, the King if you will. He has his main pieces: a rook, a bishop, a knight, and a queen. Those are the most important pieces to the main player and the most powerful. Each of the five pieces represents a borough and there's a head man who is called a Piece to run it. You follow?

"I'm following." Sheila doesn't take her eyes off her cousin for a second. She is completely focused.

"Now under each Piece, you have a group of smaller players that usually consists of about three to five men or as many as they want. But they hardly do over five. The Piece for that borough breaks their borough down into regions and distributes it among the players. It's the players' responsibility to run that district and collect the revenue and turn it in to their Piece and the Piece turns his profit into the King which is the big boss. The players get their cut, the Piece gets his and the King gets the rest."

"How much do they profit?"

"Who?"

"The players…"

"When the bookkeeper comes in and does the math, we can walk away with over a hundred thousand dollars over a two-week period. But a lot of that goes back into product, paying the people who work for you—who by the way are called pawns."

"…pawns?"

"Yeah, foot soldiers, the expendable ones…the ones who hang out on the street corners selling product."

Sheila nods.

"So, tell me how this mess came about last night. Who's after Ruby?"

"My boss, one of the main Pieces, is after her. I didn't know this, but Ruby's real father is…"

"…a drug dealer, right?"

"Yeah, but he ain't no regular drug dealer, he is *the* head honcho in charge, the big man up top, He's the King I've been explaining to you. How did you know that, anyway?"

"Sean told me."

"That dude, man…he's in trouble too. Tony wants him dead just as much as Ruby and he won't stop 'til it's done."

"Ok," Sheila shakes her head as she senses them getting off track. "What happened *last night*?"

"Aight, Tony, who is my boss, called us in for a

meeting and told us that the King pin wants to send all of us out to find his daughter, but he wanted us to do something different. Apparently, he's always had this secret beef with the man and he saw this as an opportunity to stage a takeover."

"By doing what?"

"Two things. One, by eliminating his direct competition, which is Sean, because he's convinced Sean has been chosen to run the business once Ruby's dad steps down and two, by threatening to kill Ruby *if* her father doesn't step down. Ruby is his Ace card. Tony knows that Rube is the King's true weakness. I think he wants to kill Sean because he just doesn't like him. I personally think he plans to kill them anyway."

"Who, Sean and Ruby?"

"Nah, Sean, Ruby, *and* her father. Her father's name is Scully. Tony sent us over to your house last night 'cause he overheard Scully giving Sean the address. He even had a picture of Ruby and it took everything in me not to..." Mike cracks his knuckles at the thought of it.

"If they had known I knew Ruby, they may have killed me right there. That's why I had to go along with it, but all I could do was text you to tell you to get out of there."

Mike rubs his face trying to work up the nerve to tell her the next part of his story.

"And Sheila…"

Sheila locks eyes with his and sees that they're suddenly apologetic…and moist.

"…I'm so sorry not to have believed you, but you were right about the guys in the hoodies. Tony admitted to committing a murder years ago around the time of your dad's death and described the entire crime scene as if it happened yesterday. It was him, Shells, I think he murdered your dad."

Sheila falls backwards into her chair, hard. This is way too much. They're all in way over their heads—her, Mike, Ruby…she places her hands over her face and closes her eyes. The tears refuse to be contained and they spill between her fingers. The more she tries to keep from falling apart, the harder it is to keep from falling apart.

Her whole family is involved…her aunt, her uncle, both cousins…and if anything happened to them it would tear their entire family apart. And now, to know that man who is after Ruby is the same man who may have killed her father, it's too much to take.

Mike interjects, hoping the next bit of news will lighten her mood, if only for a little bit.

"Also, there's a guy who's undercover from Internal Affairs and he's one of the players in my region. He keeps a dumb low profile, literally, but he revealed himself to me when he noticed me texting and walking around the outside of your house wasting time. I don't know, but I kind of trust him, and you know how I feel about 5-0."

Sheila can't believe it.

"I'm working with a captain from the precinct I used to intern at and he's helping me too. He told me that Internal Affairs was in on it but I had no idea they were really *in* on it! Wait 'til I tell him that they actually have a man in there undercover."

"Oh good, so, is that where you're staying, with him? He's keeping you and Ruby safe, right? You need a man that knows how to discharge a weapon, especially with all this going on." Mike exhales, relieved to know that his cousins are safe and protected.

"Actually, Ruby ran away this afternoon. She was pissed about us trying to take her back to Jersey to get her out of here, but we wouldn't take no for an answer. So, she left."

"Where's Sean? Do you think she went out with him?"

"No, he spent the night last night too 'cause he couldn't go home either, but he bounced this morning. I think he's overwhelmed too and I don't blame him. David thinks he left so that Ruby wouldn't feel the need to stay."

"Do you know where she went?"

"I don't know, but I'm thinking she may have tried to

go back to the house to get her car."

"No!" Mike jumps up from his chair alarming nearby patrons. "She can't go back there!"

"Why, what's wrong? Are those guys still there?"

"Tony has that place under 24-hour surveillance! If no one is there now, they will be, quickly! We gotta get over there!"

"Mike, I sent my boy David over there to find her. You can't go over there and blow your cover! You have to stay out of it so that we know what his next moves are."

"Sheila, NO! You don't understand! You have no idea what they plan to do to her if they get their hands on her. We have to go get her now! We can't even let Tony's men get close to her!"

"Mike, David will get there and hopefully he'll find her. Let's hope we're wrong and she went somewhere else but if you run up in there and expose yourself, they'll want you dead too and not only will I be devastated, but we won't know what his next moves are. We have to be smart about this! If anything, David is a cop and he can call for backup. We can't."

Mike is shaking, still not wanting to do what Sheila is telling him to do, but he has to face the truth.

"As much as I don't want to listen to you, 'cause you

don't know them better than I do, *Sheila*," he says annoyed. "You're right. I can't help her if I'm dead too."

"Mike, we have to strategize and work with what we have. You are on the inside along with the guy from Internal Affairs and we can use that to our advantage. This guy is playing a dangerous game and it's about time someone backed *him* into a corner."

Chapter 13

Splinters of pain shoot through Tony's hand and wrist. He should probably stop. Perhaps take a break. He's been at it for hours without having as much as a glass of water to quench his thirst.

A snap of the fingers brings an icy, perspiring glass his way, compliments of one of his most loyal players, Hakim. In a few gulps the water is gone.

"You've been working up a sweat, man. You sure you don't want to stop for a little while longer?" says Hakim.

"No, just refill this for me and bring me a glass of scotch on the rocks when you're done."

"Aight, what about your shoes? You want me to take them to get cleaned? You have, um, you have a stain on 'em."

Tony looks down at his shoes. They're the cream suede loafers his wife had given him for their anniversary last year, an expensive memento to celebrate his accomplishments as an amazing father, a supportive husband and provider. It was the gesture that spoke to him: no one can walk in his footsteps. No one has the balls to fill his shoes, nor could they. It warmed his heart to know that his family actually appreciates him. In a thankless industry like this, it's easy to be forgotten, overlooked...replaced.

He slowly steps out of them one by one.

"You can just get rid of these. I don't think it's gonna come out."

Hakim admires them for a moment, then drops them onto the clear plastic tarp covering the floor for disposal. It's a shame to see that perfect pair of shoes go to waste. A pair like those could easily go for a couple thousand dollars, he thinks. He returns to his seat by the door, arms folded in disappointment.

"If he didn't want them, he could've just given them to me. I would've scrubbed the hell out of those loafers," Hakim mumbles to himself. He continues to watch Tony interrogate some poor guy who had been in the wrong place at the wrong time.

Tony walks barefoot slowly across the tarp, hardly avoiding the large puddles of blood that had gathered in the creases and folds of the plastic. He doesn't mind the squishing beneath his feet. He glances behind him, admiring the bloody trail of horror left in his path.

His victim wheezes and coughs, spitting up blood between desperate gasps for air. His eyes are nearly swollen shut and his jaw aches to the touch, perhaps it's broken. His arms have lost most mobility. His left arm had been dislocated in the scuffle and the right arm had been broken only minutes before.

The man had drifted in and out of consciousness throughout the night, which was the only relief he had against the excruciating pain he was suffering. On a few occasions he had awoken to these complete strangers wailing on him, kicking him in his face and chest. Before he passed out, breathing wasn't an issue but after opening his eyes again for the fourth time, it seemed to be the only thing his mind could focus on. They must have broken his ribs.

Why is this happening?

Tony slaps him, trying to wake him up. Perhaps a splash of cold water will do the trick, he thinks, as he empties a bucket of water onto his face and slaps him even harder. When the man finally comes to, the pain is unbearable. He can hardly recognize his own voice as he screams in agony. There's blood everywhere. So much of it. It pours from every wound, forming a moat of crimson red around him. The moat seems to grow larger by the second as he tries to apply pressure to a deep laceration in his waist. He screams again as he shifts his weight onto his broken arm. Tears race down his black and blue face diluting the blood streaming from his nose. It's broken and it hurts like hell. He takes a painful gasp of air.

"Ah, look who's awake and trying to talk," Tony laughs. "What are you trying to say, huh? What is it? I'm giving you a break since you keep falling asleep. But just know this: we'll get nowhere if you keep taking naps."

Malcolm, who'd just arrived, approached Tony, ignoring Hakim's warning to stay back.

"Hey boss, the last of the shipments is done. Told management to take off early and close the loading docks for the night. We'll have the warehouse to ourselves. I told them we were having a meeting back here and not to disturb us. That fat annoying as hell supervisor you got down there on the floor was trying to give me a hard time, talking about shipments coming in from Florida, but I told him--"

"I don't *care* what you told him. He's gone, right? Everybody's gone?" Tony scolds him.

"Yeah…"

"Ok, that's all I needed to know. Don't you see me working here?"

Malcolm rolls his eyes and retreats to stand by the door next to Hakim.

"I hate when I go out of my way to please this dude and he acts like he don't appreciate anything I do," Malcom complains.

"At least you're not fetching him water like a slave, like me. Got me running back and forth to the sink like I'm some house negro," Hakim replies.

"Wait, Tony don't drink tap."

"He drinkin' that tap today, screw that."

Malcom grins, but it fades quickly as he watches his boss flex his authority over his victim.

"I'm tired of him talking down to us, man. I can't wait 'til we find this girl so I can finally be what I was born to be."

"And what's that?" Hakim asks.

"A Piece."

The man on the floor coughs and swallows hard.

"What do you want from me?!" he screams.

Without a second thought, Malcolm runs to the center of the room and kicks him hard in the stomach, venting his anger on the already beaten victim. The man doubles over in pain and spits out more blood. A few teeth follow but it doesn't matter. He rubs his tongue along the top gumline of his mouth and finds that five of his front teeth are already missing; a few more doesn't make a difference.

"Malcolm!" Tony quickly straightens up from kneeling. "Can you give it a rest already? How am I supposed to get anything out of him if he's unconscious? I got this!"

"My bad," replies Malcolm. "I just didn't like the way

he was talking to you," Malcolm lies.

Hakim laughs from the doorway until Tony shoots him a scathing look. Tony turns his attention back to the bloody mangled mess that lays before him.

"I told you before, I'm looking for someone and I think you know how to find him."

His victim looks up with his one decent eye, trying to focus on his captor.

"What makes you think... I know who you're looking for?" he struggles to say.

"...because my boys saw you knocking on his door and yelling his name," Tony smiles.

The man on the floor shifts a bit, wincing in pain, suddenly feeling a sense of panic.

"What were you doing there, and tell me the truth because if you don't, I'll have my friends over there cut your fingers off."

Through bloodshot eyes, the man looks towards the door and sees Hakim holding a pair of sharp clippers.

"And if you still don't tell us and there are no more fingers left, we'll start looking for other things to cut off," Tony pats the area between the man's legs. The young man tries to sit up straight.

"I, um, just went by to get some money from him that

he owed a friend of mine. I really don't know him like that..."

Tony shakes his head.

"Lies!"

Tony smacks him with such force that the back of his hand stings with pain.

"Aye, Tony! Look at what I found in ol' boy's phone!" says Malcolm.

"WHAT! He was just about to tell me something and you're interrupting! Do you want your fingers cut off too?"

Malcolm sucks his teeth. "He knows him, just like we thought. He sent this guy mad text messages before we found him and look at what it says!" He tosses Tony the phone and as he reads the messages his mouth turns up into a smile.

"Oh, this just keeps on getting better and better," Tony laughs. He bends down again to speak to the guy on the floor, who continues to twist and turn in pain.

"You should have just told me the truth. Hakim, come over here and show us how we deal with liars!"

Instantly, Hakim is out of his seat and quickly walking towards the group of men. He grabs the man's hand and places his index finger between the blades of the clippers.

"Count to three," Hakim demands.

"One..." the man on the floor hears the snap of the clippers closing and feels the burning sensation shoot through his hand and up his entire arm.

"Ahhhhhhh! My God! My...my finger!" he cries.

"Now," says Tony, "now that I know who you are, you are going to make a phone call and tell him where he can come and get you." He looks down at the bloody hand with mangled flesh hanging from the stub of the severed finger.

"I guess I'll have to dial that for you," Tony chuckles. The phone rings and Tony put it to the man's face. "Tell him you're at 23 Mason Avenue and if he's not here in two hours you're dead."

The phone continues to ring and just as Tony is about to hang up...

"Hello...?"

"Sean," he winces in pain, "please...come get me, man, they said they're gonna kill me."

"What...who...where are you?"

"23 Mason Avenue. We're at your old job, hurry! They said you only have two hours!"

The line cuts off. Sean stares at the phone in horror. He listens again, hoping his brother was still on the line.

"Damian...DAMIAN!"

A KING'S RANSOM

Chapter 14

Ruby walks up the familiar block towards Sheila's house, breathing a sigh of relief. Her car is still in the driveway, untouched. She takes in her surroundings to see if anyone had followed her and when she feels confident enough; she approaches her car. Everything is as she'd left it. The tank is full, an old fountain drink still sits in the cup holder and an old parking ticket lay on the passenger seat, which reminds her, she needs to pay that.

Something moves, she thinks, but a quick scan reveals nothing. Standing outside, alone in the dark with nothing but the dim indoor lights of her car, suddenly doesn't feel very safe. Ruby reaches into her pocket to feel the coolness of the can of pepper spray the old woman had given her. Even if she doesn't use it, the fact that she has it at her fingertips puts her mind at ease, at least for a little while.

As she begins to get inside of the car, she realizes she'd been wearing the same clothes for two days straight. She had fresh laundry in the house, she's sure to find something clean to put on before she heads back out again.

Going against her better judgment, Ruby leaves the security of her vehicle and approaches the house. It's dark outside, darker than she thought she'd ever seen it. The lights are off in the house, which is a rare sight. The whole neighborhood felt…dark.

The street lights hardly worked at full luminosity. Many of them flickered or didn't work at all. The one working streetlight at the end of the driveway only illuminated part of the street and sent a little splash of golden glow through the living room window. As Ruby steps inside, an eerie feeling creeps over her. Her footsteps are slow and loud as the wood creaks beneath her feet. She tries to flick on the light switch by the stairwell but it won't turn on.

As she makes her way through the house, desperately trying to convince herself that Sheila hadn't paid the electric bill, she repeats this over and over in her head to make herself feel less vulnerable and idiotic for entering the house in the first place. She refuses to believe that someone had cut the power intentionally. But the closer she gets to the back hallway, the faster her heart beats.

"Why in the world did I come in here?" she whispers to herself. Everything seems like a horror movie unfolding right before her eyes. She half expects Jason to run out of her room, scaring her half to death threatening her with death by chainsaw.

Ruby laughs to herself. Jason is a fictional character.

"*There is no one in this house but me*," she reassures herself. As she opens the door to her room, she peeks inside to confirm no one is there. After a quick search for her laundry, she grabs the entire bag and leaves the room.

✱✱✱✱

Across the street, Chino lurks behind a house whose backyard lights coincidentally were out. He'd watched her walk towards her car and he began to cross the street. It was his chance to grab the girl, finally. He'd been following her for a couple of hours now, texting his ETA to Tony every now and then, letting him know where he was and how close he was to his target.

Earlier that night, Chino had been making a transaction on his block when a bus pulled up right in front of him. Imagine his surprise when he saw the very girl he and his cronies were looking for, on the bus! They all thought it was hilarious that Scully wanted them to call him if they *happened* to see her. It just didn't make any sense, who does that? Who *just so happens* to see the very girl they had been sent to look for, who could have been hiding anywhere in the tri-state.

Chino couldn't believe his eyes. He hurried with his exchange and ran for the bus. He'd almost missed it but luckily the bus stopped just in time.

After he verified that it was her, he texted news of his recent discovery to his head of operations. He might get a promotion after this, he thought. How lucky for him that he could help put his boss' great plan into action! After he'd settled into his seat, he was able to keep a good eye on her and every move she made but, there was one problem. He couldn't help staring at her! She was a twenty out of ten!

The picture Tony gave them did her no justice. The attraction he felt to her was so great, his loins began to do a dance of their own, little to his surprise. On few occasions, she caught him staring and he would quickly look away. He didn't want to bring too much attention to himself but he couldn't help it.

The little old woman kept watching him, which annoyed him to high hell. He couldn't stand her little piercing eyes and felt relieved when she struck up a conversation with the girl. He used that time to call Tony and ask him what he should do next. When he had been given his orders, he contemplated the best way to fulfill them.

As he followed her off of the bus and onto the train, he predicted that she was going back to the house where they had searched for her the night before. He communicated with his boss throughout the short trip to the house. Tony was going to send backup his way and told him to wait tight, but if she looked like she was going to get away, he was to do anything he could do to keep her there.

Chino smiled to himself; he had just the thing in mind. But then, as he stalked across the street, she jumped out of her Mercedes-Benz and looked around. He ducked behind a nearby tree and hid in the shadows just in time; she hadn't seen him. She walked up the lawn and into the house.

"Dammit," he said to himself. "That was too close. Maybe I should just wait for backup to get here," he thought.

****

Walking back towards the front door, Ruby doesn't feel as scared as she did when she first entered the house. She has no worries until she reaches the front door, and a large callused hand clamps across her mouth from behind. She's violently dragged backwards further into the house. She struggles, dropping her bag of clothes onto the floor, jumping up and down, trying to break free of her assailant's grasp. She can breathe just fine because the hands aren't covering her entire face but the panic triggers terror within her nonetheless.

Ruby stomps on the man's feet and claws at his face to no avail. She jams her elbow deep into his gut, constantly trying to get free but his hold on her doesn't let up. It seems he's more concerned with keeping her quiet than fighting her.

She pushes herself backwards so that they both hit the wall. She finally feels his grip loosen. Another swift elbow to the gut releases her and she digs into her pockets as he's bent over trying to catch his breath. She quickly pulls out the pepper spray, hoses him down, letting her finger rest on the nozzle until she's convinced the spray has run out. He coughs but he isn't reacting to the spray like she'd hoped.

"Ruby, please STOP, STOP..." he manages to say while still coughing. He runs to the kitchen to wash his eyes out and puts his head inside the sink to let the faucet run over his entire face. Ruby is afraid to move but her curiosity always betrays her.

This person had said her name and didn't put up much of a fight at all. She would like to think that she could fight off someone three times her size, but the reality is, she couldn't. It was too easy for him to overpower her. Plus, he obviously knows the house well enough to know where the kitchen is.

She quietly follows behind him. He grabs a towel to dry his face.

"Ruby, don't say anything…it's me, David."

"David!" Ruby screams.

"Shhhh!" He quickly walks over to her.

"David, what are you doing here?" She whispers.

"I came here to get you and good thing I did," he says, walking to the window to peek through the side of the curtains.

"Why, what's going on?"

"When I rolled up the block, I saw someone following you. He was hiding behind that house across the street and he looked like he was on the phone."

"Oh my god! Did he have on a black sweatshirt?"

"A black hoodie is more like it," David replies as he makes his way back to her. "Are you ok? I didn't hurt you, did I?"

"No, but why did you have to do all of that? Couldn't you have just said who you were?"

"Ruby, they're watching the house and I didn't know who was in here with you. I didn't want to alarm them if they'd already gotten to you. I needed you to stay as quiet as possible because I'm pretty sure they saw me enter the house."

"So, what do we do now?" she asks, terrified.

"I have to get you out of here, that's the most important thing. Do you have any more of that spray left?"

"I don't think so, but I don't think it worked. It must be old. It didn't have any effect on you."

David rolls his eyes.

"Ruby that spray ..."

She holds back an inappropriate giggle. "Oh, 'cause you didn't look like you were..."

"I'm a cop, Ruby. I'm used to pepper spray, but it's still pepper spray," David says, annoyed. "Anyway, we're gonna go out the side door, but stay close behind me. There was only one of them when I pulled up but he may have called for backup already."

"David, I'm scared, what are we gonna do?"

"Just follow close and don't say anything. If something happens just run off into the other direction, I'll catch up with you later."

"David, what are you talking about, you'll catch up with me..."

"Ruby, shhh...before they hear you!" They quietly walk outside and around the side of the house, carefully stepping over a trash can lid and garden tools. As they approach the clearing, David scans the area and slowly takes out his weapon.

"Look, I parked down the street. Can you see the car from here?"

Ruby looks over his shoulder in the direction he's facing. She sees the car but isn't sure how they could possibly make it that far without being seen.

"I see it," she whispers, "but how…"

"Shhh, just follow me," says David. They make their way down the driveway and kneel behind Ruby's car.

"Can't we just get in here?" she asks.

"Do you have the key on you?"

"Yeah, let me just get it out of my pocket." As Ruby reaches into her pants, David suddenly lunges in her direction.

David tackles the man in the black hoodie, who had crept behind them! Ruby screams and fumbles in her pockets for the spray can as the two men tussle on the pavement. She tries to aim her can directly at the man but she can't get a clean shot without hitting David again.

"Ruby, run!" David seems to be overpowering his opponent but things quickly go from bad to worse. The mysterious assailant kicks him hard in the face, sending him into a daze for a few moments, unable to tell which way is which. The hooded man then turns his attention to Ruby but she's already scrambling backwards on all fours. Too overcome with shock to stand upright and run for her life, she finally finds her footing and leaps out into the street and begins to sprint down the block.

David's car is still running and if she can just get to it, she has a chance to escape. But she can't just leave David there like that. She glances back to see about David and sees their attacker is chasing her and closing in on her heels. In fact, he's much closer than she expected. Her adrenaline kicks up a notch as she realizes she'll never make it to David's car. Just as he reaches out to grab her, she hears David yell, "Freeze!" But the man doesn't stop, which forces her to keep running.

David drew his weapon and although the man is running, Ruby is convinced that David would be able to make the shot. Then, she hears it ring out into the darkness. Pop, pop!

She turns around again. The hooded man is still chasing her and this time he's right on top of her. He tackles her and pins her on the ground with her hands behind her back. He stuffs a dirty rag into her mouth. It tastes like vinegar and smells like gym socks.

How in the world is he still standing, she thinks? She's sure David had shot him twice! Now her heart is in her throat, her body and hands trembling uncontrollably.

"Don't be scared, pretty lady," Chino whispers into her ear. He straddles her in the middle of the street as she lies face down on the concrete. He leans in to get closer so that she can hear him more easily, and when he does, he receives a whiff of the most delicious scent he'd ever smelled. It was a cool mixture of flowers, vanilla, and citrus, with strong undertones of fear and terror. As he strokes her long locks, he becomes entranced by her soft skin and her beautiful features.

"Ahhhh," he whispers again.

"You are...so...fine...I...I," he can't even get his words out.

His lower region becomes stiffer by the second as he grinds himself up and down the crease of her backside to keep her from wriggling away. Tears stream down her face as he violates her but there's nothing she can do to get away. She tries to fight, but the harder she fights, the more he moves, pushing her pinned arms higher and higher behind her until she feels they might break.

Ruby's screams are muffled by the dirty sock lodged tightly in her mouth. She has to stop moving for fear that she'll run out of breath or that her arms will break. Chino notices her tears and bends down again to try and calm her down.

"Don't worry...I'm gonna take good care of you." His

lips were so close to her face, the funk from his breath made it unbearable to breathe what little air she could; she thought she would pass out from that alone. Chino is mesmerized by her fear. It makes him feel powerful. He licks the tears on her face slowly, one by one. Ruby struggles even harder.

Where is David, she screams internally. She wants to yell for help so that someone, anyone, could hear and call the police, but she can't. She's helpless. Just then, a black Honda rolls up on them and screeches to a halt.

"Yo, what is you doin'?" yells Hakim. "Get the hell in the car, we gotta go now!"

Chino yanks Ruby up off of the cold street. She mumbles and tries to break free as he desperately tries to stuff her in the car. To his surprise, she won't go without a fight. She kicks and screams, wedging her feet on both sides of the car door as he tries to push her in. Hakim gets out of the car to give him a hand.

"Yo, man, you playin' with this chick," he says. "Knock her out and let's go!"

"Look, don't tell me how to do this, I do this all the time. I-," Hakim has had enough and punches Ruby so hard in the back of her head that her body collapses into their arms. Hakim shoves her inside, slams the door behind her, and runs back to the driver's seat.

"Why the...I had it!" yells Chino.

"Cause you was bs'in'. Now we don't have to listen to her strugglin' all the way back." Chino watches her swoon from the blow. He reaches back and ties her hands together with plastic ties as he takes in every inch of her body, resting his eyes on her breasts, taking in the fullness and shape of them.

This will make things a lot easier, he thinks.

"Besides," says Hakim, "if I hadn't shown up in time, you would be one dead motha... I got that dude twice before he even got one shot off."

"Whatever," says Chino. "I knew what I was doin."

Ruby leans her head up against the cold window as they pass the house. The last image she sees is David lying on his back in the middle of the lawn.

"David..."

****

Sheila slams on the brakes while heading down a one-way street, missing a head-on collision by inches. Cars honk and drivers curse at her as she flies down a residential block towards the parkway. She has to get to her house and quick.

God, please let me get there in time.

David had been shot and it was the last thing she expected to hear. She hoped he would tell her that he'd found Ruby and that she was ok, but instead he told her that he'd been shot twice and they took her cousin away in a black Honda. It's a miracle that he'd worn his Kevlar vest when he went in search for Ruby! Had he not, he probably would've been dead.

Sheila tries to keep calm but everything about her is starting to unravel. She suppresses an oncoming anxiety attack, forcing herself to remain calm, but easier said than done. Both of her cousins are in extreme danger and her friend, her lover, had been attacked in the process and shot, left for dead. How can she focus? Every time she thinks about it, about them, her stomach twists and plummets.

I can't do this by myself anymore, she thinks. *I need help.*

Chapter 15

"Damn…"

Scully tilts his head back and closes his eyes as he pumps himself again and again into a wailing prostitute. She screams and whines for him to do it harder, but even with her years of experience, she doesn't think she can take it much longer. With every thrust she feels like he's tearing her apart, but she dares not tell him. She's never had a dissatisfied customer and she doesn't want to start now. His money is really good and every girl on the block knows it.

"Lucky trick…" she heard them mumble as she slid into the car and sat next to the infamous Scully. He hadn't been around these parts for a long time. He used to do business with the pimps in this area, setting up old hoes with work and making sure they were treated properly.

Word on the street is he'd stopped inviting girls to his place. He had one for every day of the week but he never picked from the streets. He wanted elite women, the ones that hung out in cigar lounges, the escorts that entertained men with power.

A long time ago, she was one of those women. She was beautiful, polished, well-mannered and in high demand.

The local New York politicians couldn't get enough of her, they'd have to coordinate their schedules just to fit her in.

That was all before the drugs and after a while, she'd accumulated so many miles, she struggled to get work. The only way she could eat was to go to where once-prized "ladies of the night" go to die: the streets.

Scully is an old customer. He used to get off by watching her entertain these politicians over dinner and drinks in some of the most expensive restaurants in the city, but by night's end she'd end up in his bed screaming his name 'til sunrise. She always suspected Scully used her to build relationships with these men, to further his influence in the city, but she had more money than she knew what to do with. Why complain?

Though, once she began to use heroine against his wishes, their partnership was never the same. Those were the good old days. She wouldn't be surprised if he'd found someone, the way he dropped her like the bad habit she was. He was addicted to her, and at that time, she was addicted to him...more-so to his wallet.

She'd be crazy to let a little pain ruin her chances to get a taste of that wealth just one more time. She could get off the streets early tonight! She's tired, a chick deserves a break.

"You like that, you like that?" Scully grunts.

"Yeah daddy, give it to me harder, do that baby, do it!!!"

He grabs her waist and forces her hips backwards to get a better angle deep inside of her. From behind, he can't see her biting her lips to keep from crying out in pain. They'd been going at it for almost an hour and usually most of her clients didn't last past ten to fifteen minutes at the most.

Scully yanks her hair and pulls it back harder than she expects. She winces but he keeps going. He's screwing her so violently she's sure she'll be bleeding by nights end.

"Is that what you want? Huh? Huh?" he yells, "HUH!?"

"No, stop it, stop it!" she screams. Tears spill from the corners of her eyes from the throbbing pain on her scalp and between her legs. She can't help it. He's about to rip her lady parts to shreds! He slows down a bit and slaps her on the behind as hard as he can. In five short strokes he ejaculates inside of her and she slides off of the bed and escapes to the bathroom.

The door slams behind her and he lies back on the pillows, out of breath. He'd had too much to drink and the liquor bottles scattered around the hotel room floor prove it.

How did I end up here, he thinks. *How did I get to this point?*

He'd left home frustrated and angry at Terry, lost and terrified for his daughter and now he's lying on the bed, completely naked and covered in sweat.

My only hope for my daughter bailed on me and I have no idea what to do next. I can't just run out in the streets looking for her alone! I have enemies! They'll follow me straight to her. And if I do find her, what do I do? What do I say? "Ruby, I'm your father. Let's go"? She probably wouldn't believe me anyway.

Scully remembers the way she stared at him the night of the wedding. It was as if the world was still and the music in the halls had gone silent. His breath was taken away and his chest tightened with excitement at the sight of his baby girl, in the flesh. Ruby locked eyes with him, staring through him as if searching for answers but he could tell she didn't know what to say or why she felt the need to say anything at all. He was speechless and so was she. The sudden urge to run to her and hold her in his arms was overwhelming.

It had been years since he'd seen her. He couldn't believe that his little girl had grown into such a beautiful young woman. He stared at her, his daughter, his little girl, and she reminded him of the woman he had never fallen out of love with. She was almost an exact spitting image, but he could see that she inherited his charming smile and deep dimples.

He'd never experienced anything like it before. It was amazing. The feeling he had as he stood there on the landing watching his own flesh and blood, moving, talking, and breathing was…surreal. All of those years he'd only had an old picture of his daughter, a distant memory of a little five-year-old girl playing with her dolls and falling asleep in her mother's lap.

A rush of happiness and an incredible amount of excitement shot through him instantly upon laying eyes on her. But he also felt a heavy heart, saddened by the thought of never being able to be the father that he'd always wanted to be. This time he won't let her go so easily. When he finds her, he's going to make sure he's a part of her life whether her mother or Jerome want it or not.

Scully shakes his head and wipes his eyes aggressively. The thought of leaving Terry the way he did, angry, confused and hurt…it eats at him. But right now, he can't face her. He can't deal with her saying, "I told you so." Even though she probably won't, he knows she'll be thinking it. He had every intention of going back home that night but after drinking beer after beer, alone in his Bentley, he decided to take it down at a hotel in Long Island. He needs this time to himself, to think, to plan to…to what else?

What else do I need to do, he ponders. *What else can I do? I've failed my family...they don't deserve me, Terry doesn't deserve me.*

His thoughts continue to spiral.

I had Terry hanging on to an idea that we had something special while I had sex with other women...with her lying in the same bed! The shame overcomes him like a tidal wave. His chest feels like it's caving in.

This woman loves me and I have love for her, but I hoped... I hoped that if I didn't show her the love she craved, she would leave just like everyone else. But she stayed. She stayed! I broke her heart and she endured it.

Scully remembers hearing her crying in the bathroom a few times. He didn't need to know why she was upset, he already knew. She was devastated because she knew she could never have him the way she wanted. He'd even made her get three abortions because he was too selfish to face his responsibilities. Never caring about her feelings and what it did to her emotionally. Scully didn't want any children, he couldn't even be a father to the one he had. He was an empty shell. He didn't know how to love anything anymore.

Scully reminisces about Marcia. She was the love of his life. Even after all these years, he still loves her even though she's married to his best friend. He remembers all the good times they shared and with them, the bad times, but one thing he can say about her is that even though she and Terry share similar characteristics, Marcia has more boundaries. She would never have allowed him to sleep with her and another woman for his pleasure.

Marcia damn near shot a girl in the face after she walked in on him cheating on her. She hated even knowing that he was messing around and she let him know it. He knew better than to ask her to join in. She would have shot *him*, no doubt about it.

Scully chuckles a bit, grateful for the memory to help lighten his mood. The mother of his child, the truest ride or die that ever was. He misses her tremendously and seeing her in her wedding gown over a month ago sent shivers up his spine and a knife through his heart. Even after all these years, he was surprised to realize that he still felt the same way about her.

Is it possible to love two people at once, he wonders? *How can I have so much love for Terry, when I still have an undying unconditional love for Marcia Matthews?*

Jerome, his best friend, his ace, his right-hand man, is now married to the woman he loved. The woman he *loves*.

Why the hell did I push them away?

He lived most of his life jealous and envious of Jerome

but what could he do? He had a business to run. He realized that Jerome saw his girls more than he did, since he sent Jerome away to watch over and protect them. It wasn't hard to understand how they became so close.

Through all of the arguments and fistfights he and Jerome had over Marcia and Ruby, he finally allowed himself to step back and let his friend pursue his woman. Besides, Jerome was right: just because he chose to do what he does, doesn't mean that everyone else had to suffer because of it. Marcia deserved someone to love and for them to love her back, and Ruby deserved a father.

If Scully relinquished the responsibility, then he should just step down and let Jerome pick up where he left off. If no other man can have her, let him take on that role. Jerome finished by saying, "At least she'll be with someone you know and you know that your family is safe with me."

Earlier that evening, after he'd checked into his hotel room on Long Island and downed half a bottle of scotch, he looked up an old friend. He knew she worked in the area and wouldn't deny him her company. Now she's in the shower wishing she'd never answered his call.

Her lady parts are sore and swollen. When she wipes herself after a burning piss, she isn't surprised to see that she was bleeding.

"Damnit," she says under her breath as she cleans herself up. She sucks her teeth as she steps into a fresh pair of underwear she pulled from her purse. She doesn't have any panty liners or anything to catch the droplets of blood so she reaches for the roll of tissue and proceeds to roll up a wad. She's so sore, yet it's still so early. There is no way she can take any more customers tonight. Scully better come up on some major cash.

She opens the bathroom door and walks back into the room to find Scully in the same spot she'd left him.

"Aight that'll be five hundred," she says as she hoists on her jacket.

"Five hundred!"

"Yeah, five hundred, Scully. Like I said. You nailed me so hard my damn vagina looks like it was in a fight! I can't work for the rest of the night because of you!"

He wants to laugh, the way she's standing there like she has something shoved up her butt, but she's right. He'd put her through enough tonight but he didn't mean to make her bleed. He reaches over to his wallet and pulls out some cash.

"I still think five hundred is too much but, here take this. That should be enough."

She sorts through a few thousand dollars in cash and

stuffs it in her bra. Without a smile or a grin, she proceeds to the door but hesitates before leaving.

"You know, life gets rough sometimes, Scully. I can testify to that. And if it wasn't for you, who knows where I would be today. The way you set me up with a place to live after my life fell apart...the way you made sure I was safe on these streets after those pimps tried to..." She's suddenly overcome with emotion.

"I never said thank you and I'm sorry."

Scully stares at the floor in front of him, beer cans clouding his peripheral vision.

"I don't know what's happened to you but I recognize pain when I see it. I know depression very well, trust me." She opens the door and looks back at her old friend. "If this is who you are now, then you've already lost. If not, there might be a sliver of hope for you yet. How 'bout you do what I failed to do and take the advice you once gave me."

The door shuts behind her and Scully is frozen in place. His life is hitting rock bottom if a prostitute has to give *him* advice, even if it was his own. As he begins to head into the bathroom, his phone rings.

"Hello?"

"Scully, it's...it's Sean. I need your help!"

"Sean!" he yells. "You have some nerve calling me! I

can't believe…"

"Scully! I'm in trouble, man! You're the only one that can help me!"

"What makes you think that I would want to help you? I asked you to do one simple thing for me and you couldn't do that!"

"Why should you help me?" Sean asks in disbelief. "'Cause I'm in this situation because of YOU! Whoever is after Ruby is after me too! They have my brother, man! They have my brother…please…please help me!"

Scully thinks hard about what Sean said. It's true that it's his fault the kid's in trouble. He did drag him into this but Sean also promised to protect Ruby and he didn't. He bailed on her, he bailed on him, and that's what hurt the most. He treated him like a son and thought he could trust him, but Sean proved to Scully that he couldn't.

"Why did you bail on my daughter, Sean? That's one thing I NEED to know before I do anything else. Why did you abandon her?" He's on the verge of tears and the hesitation in Sean's voice doesn't help.

"Scully, there is something I need to tell you but it's better I tell you in person."

"No! You tell me RIGHT NOW because I can't promise I won't kill you myself when I see you, and you *know*

I'm not lyin."

Sean takes a deep breath.

"This is going to sound crazy to you but...I already know...Ruby."

"What?! What do you mean you already know her?"

"I already know her...in fact, we're sort of dating."

Scully is dumbfounded.

"How, why...when...when did this all happen? How did you meet her? She doesn't even live out here!"

"About a month or so ago I went to this wedding out in Queens with my ex-girlfriend Pam and she introduced me to her friend Ruby..."

"Wait, wait...Pam...Brown?"

"Yeah, that's her. You know her, right?"

"Well yes, but I haven't seen her or her family for years, but go ahead," Scully encourages him.

"When I walked her to her car the night of the wedding, she almost got carjacked and kidnapped but I was there and fought them off. We kept in touch after that. I met you soon after but I had no idea that you two were related until you showed me her picture a few days ago and told me what was happening. I was completely shocked and I didn't know what to do! You sent me over there that night but I was already invited there for dinner. It felt weird and awkward, man. The crazy part is, someone was on their way over there too…to do God knows what to her and her family. But her cousin Sheila got a message from her cousin Mike to leave the house because his people were on their way…"

"Sheila and Mike," Scully whispers, reminiscing on his earlier life with Marcia and her sisters' children. Marcia loved her family so much, she could always be found at their houses babysitting the both of them. They were an inseperable family back then but all of that had changed, because of him.

"We went to a friend of Sheila's and that's where she told me that someone was after both me and Ruby."

Sean takes another deep breath.

"I love your daughter, man. More than anything else in this world and when she told me she felt the same, Scully, I have to admit that I was scared. This whole thing with someone trying to kill her makes me sick! Sheila kept telling her to go back home to Jersey where she would be safe but she wouldn't. She had a reason to stay out here and I didn't want to be that reason." Sean wipes his eyes and swallows hard as he relives his hard decision to leave her.

"I figured if I left her, she would be angry enough to go back home, but I couldn't deal with living without her, or being surrounded by things that reminded me of her, which is why I had to stop dealing with you too. Do you understand? In order for her to live I had to leave!"

Scully knows exactly how he feels and if he wasn't convinced that Sean shared the same qualities as him, he's sure of it now.

"So, will you help me save my little brother? They gave me two hours!"

"Where is Ruby?"

"Last I saw her she was with Sheila at her friend's house this morning. When I left she was fine."

"Call Sheila and get them to come to the gym in thirty minutes so at least we know Ruby's safe," says Scully.

"I don't have her number. I only have Ruby's."

"Well call Ruby then!" he yells at Sean's stupidity. The kid is so scared he can't even think straight. "Now all we need to do is rescue your brother."

"How are we gonna do that?" Sean asks frantically.

"The old man at the gym will help me figure out what to do."

Chapter 16

Terry and Marcia exit their vehicles.

"Well this isn't what I expected," says Marcia.

"What is it?" asks Terry.

"I haven't been here in years…I didn't know you were bringing me to *this* gym."

Terry follows Marcia's line of sight to a big sign with flood lights at the top of the building.

"It looks different but, it's still the same."

"Come on. Follow me inside, there's someone I'd like you meet."

The two enter the gym side by side and immediately the clinks and clangs of metal hitting metal echo throughout the gym. The huffs and groans of the men on the weight machines are like a choir of testosterone in every octave.

It's hard for Marcia not to steal a glance at these attractive men lifting ten times her weight. The sweat glistens on their chiseled bodies and their veins throb with pure untamed strength. The adrenaline rushes to her heart, quickening its beat while her lungs try desperately to keep up.

Terry begins to speak but notices Marcia entranced in a secret fantasy.

"Enjoying the view?"

Marcia blushes, quickly turning away. Terry laughs.

"No need to be shy. I don't think I could trust you if you could walk past all of that without as much as a second glance. Or a third or fourth," she says, sliding into a fantasy of her own.

Marcia rolls her eyes but not before she cracks a slight smile.

"Ain't no crime in smiling either. It's ok."

Marcia clears her throat and gives Terry her full attention. She couldn't care less about the men in this gym. It's just...watching them work out and train for a fight...it reminds her of someone. It reminds her of what she used to love most about him. His raw, undeniable strength.

"What were you about to say?" Marcia asks.

"I was about to ask you to wait here for a second. I'll be right back."

Terry enters the manager's office and closes the door behind her. Marcia stands there for a minute with her arms folded and further observes the room.

There's a lot of new equipment here. None of this was here before, she thinks.

There's a boxing ring in the middle of the floor with young men wearing blue and red "Everlast" head guards and matching gloves.

The kid in blue can use some help on his uppercut. That one in the red is comin' at him too fast. He's gonna get him with a combo. Jab-jab-cross-left hook. Jab-left hook...Blue...hit him with a right cross-left hook-right cross! Ugh...this kid is about to get an uppercut to the jaw in 3-2-1...

Blue is down on his back. *Didn't even see it comin', poor kid.*

Marcia continues to look around. Young men worked mostly on free weights and calisthenics. The older ones were on cardio. Figures. She remembers when this place was a rut. The equipment was always broken and the customers always complained. There were never as many white folks in this place as there are now. There used to be so much diversity in here; Spanish, black, white, Indian.

Gentrification at its best, I see.

She still can't believe how long she's been gone! She feels out of place. How could she be home yet feel so out of place?

"Hey ma, you came here to work out?"

Marcia spins around. A scrawny brown-skinned boy with fuzzy braids wearing an oversized shirt that says "Jim's Gym" is sizing her up and licking his li'l ashy chapped lips.

"Excuse me," she asks?

"I said, you here to work out? I could show you a li'l

somethin' if you want. I work here, you know." He smooths down his baggy gym shirt, proud to wear the brand on his chest.

"We have some of the best athletes in all the boroughs that work out here. Sometimes a few brotha's from the Nets and the Giants come here to work out too. We have private rooms for them in the basement. I can give you a tour if you want."

There goes that lip licking thing again.

"Um, no, I didn't come in here to work out." Marcia rolls her eyes and looks the other way, hoping he can take a hint.

"So, I guess that means you came in here for me. Let me get your number and…"

Marcia has heard enough. "Li'l boy, I am three times your age …"

"I'm just sayin', I like my ladies seasoned and well done, you know!"

"I'm not interested!"

"Ma, I'm sayin' though…"

"Clarence! The lady said she's not interested; didn't you hear her? I've trained you better than that. Get back to work!"

Clarence falls back but not without blowing Marcia an

air kiss. He retreats to the boxing ring and resumes picking up sweaty towels.

Marcia whips around to find Terry and the old man standing in the doorway of his office. Her heart plummets at the sight of him.

"I'm sorry," he says, "That damn kid harasses most of my customers but I assure you, he's harmless. He just needs a good firm hand is all, no father in his life, you see."

He nods his head towards Clarence and Marcia takes another look at the boy, watching him as he wipes down the benches and shadow boxes with the air in front of him. He copies the combinations of the men in the ring, watching them intently and in awe.

Marcia turns back to the old man.

"Jim," she whispers.

"Ce," he spreads his arms wide and she runs into them, almost squeezing the remaining life out of him. Everything she'd been holding onto for the past month since Ruby disappeared boils to the top and spills out of her eyes.

"It's ok, Ce Ce…it's ok," Jim whispers as he consoles her. She can't control her sobs and begins to cry heavily, drawing attention from the customers.

"Why don't we go into the office," Terry suggests, ushering them both through the doorway.

"Jim...I...I don't know what to say. It's been such a long time; it's been what, fifteen years?"

"That it has been, my dear, and the years have been good to you," he smiles.

"Oh," she sniffles, "please, Jim, I'm starting to feel my forty-something," she wipes her eyes and smiles back. "I'm not as young as I used to be."

"None of us are, honey."

Jim takes out his handkerchief and wipes her eyes for her. He'd aged too but she remembers him looking the same back then as he did now. Even when she was a teenager he looked like an old man. Stress can take its toll on the body, her mother always said.

"You're still as young, vibrant, and beautiful as you were when you were sixteen, Marcia and you probably still have the same old temper." His eyes smile.

Marcia looks towards Terry, who's busy making coffee in the corner of the room, and feels a tinge of guilt. Terry gives her a wink and a huge grin and continues brewing the coffee.

"I've been working on it," Marcia admits. "How have you been? I see the gym has come a long way since I've been gone and you look like you've been keeping in shape too." She pinches his frail arms and appears to be impressed.

"Well, I have been working out a little bit here and there you know," he flexes. A loud chuckle escapes from the corner of the room and Jim turns around to give Terry a stare of death.

She gasps, sarcastically.

"You done with my coffee yet, woman?" he teases.

"Just a sec, Jim," she says as she pounds on the coffeemaker to get the liquid to come out faster.

Jim moves a black chess piece on his board, analyzing the move he made, and quickly picks up a white piece to counter the movement. It seems he'd been playing a game of chess with himself. He's the same old Jim, Marcia notices. You can't pull this man away from this game even if you tried. It's his obsession.

After feeling satisfied with his move, he slowly looks up to see Marcia staring at him, wondering why she'd stopped talking. He gently pushes the board to the side. There are just certain things that needed to be done before he could carry on and now that he'd satisfied his itch, he can no longer be distracted. Now he can have peace of mind while he converses with an old friend. Playing chess with himself or with an opponent is the only way to suppress the dangerous urge to go back to being the person he once was. He'd played a real-life game of chess with his own life and he was great at it, but as he'd gotten older he realized the game was changing and he couldn't keep up. That's when he turned it all over to Scully.

"I see you have a new ring and better equipment...you're really doing well for yourself," Marcia continues.

Jim shifts in his chair to search for his old pipe in his back pockets. "It ain't me, you know. I didn't do all of this," he admits. "Cassius helped me out a bit. He sent me a check and I picked out everything I wanted for this place and business has been good ever since."

"Cassius. Good ol' Cassius, always lookin' out for your best interest. When it's really his and not yours," Marcia avoids eye contact with Jim.

"Now, now, don't be like that, Marci. Cassius always had your best interest at heart. Don't think like that."

Talking to Jim was like talking to her grandfather. He speaks slowly and cautiously so that you understand his every word, yet he has a comforting demeanor about him. The respect she has for Jim is like that of a father, but there were times when she disagreed even with her own father.

Terry brings them both a cup of coffee and goes back to the corner to take a seat away from the couple. This is an intimate conversation that has nothing to do with her. She did her part by bringing Marcia here and now she has to blend in with the walls so the two can talk peacefully without being distracted. She wants to hear everything. She wants to know Cassius' story so that she can connect the dots and see his future more clearly. Everything she knew about him was only what he wanted her to know and it bothered her. It's always bothered her. In the little bit of time that she's known Marcia, she learned more things about Cassius in five minutes than in her whole eight years of being with him. She sips from her cup and waits for Marcia to speak.

"How can you say that, Jim? How can you say that he was looking out for me when he almost ruined my entire life?" Marcia asks.

"Is it ruined now?" he asks as he puffs on his pipe.

"No, but..."

"Then you can't blame someone for *almost* ruining your life, if they never succeeded in the first place."

Marcia takes a long sip from her mug and places it gently on the table. She ponders what the old man said and although it makes sense, it doesn't make her feel any better.

"Ok, Jim, so why do I have all of this anger inside of me? Why does it still hurt when I think about how he sent me away and kept me from seeing my family for all of those years? How come I still think about the day my friend was murdered right in front of me, RIGHT IN FRONT OF ME? I

236

can't help but blame it all on him. If he were never in this business she might still be alive today! No one would've come after him. They wouldn't have come to the house and Patricia would still be alive!"

Jim watches her as she grows more emotional by the second. "If you want to know why you are so angry, you should ask yourself."

"What? What are you talking about?"

"When Cassius sent you away from your family, who prevented you from seeing them?"

"He did…"

"No Marci, you did. You stayed away on your own."

"But he told me to, Jim, he told me to stay away because of *his* enemies…"

"I'm not saying he had nothing to do with it, but *no one* should be able to keep you away from the people you love, no one, not even Cassius. If you felt it was so dangerous, then why didn't you invite them to join you where you were, sooner?"

"It was too hard to explain to them why I couldn't come home. I couldn't tell them anything because they didn't know the type of lifestyle he lived," Marcia tries to explain.

"You mean the type of lifestyle you *both* lived, Marcia. You see, it's much easier to blame someone else for everything than to take responsibility for your share in it."

"Jim! Are you kidding me? It's all because of him! What about Patricia? She's dead because of him. I think about her all the time…all the time and it hurts so much…I…"

"Does it hurt because of what you did?"

"Huh?" Both Marcia and Terry are laser focused on Jim. It seems as if the old man is making excuses for Cassius. "What *I* did?" she yells.

"Yes, child, what you did. You see, Cassius didn't pull the trigger, Marci, so you can't blame him for that. Cassius and JT killed the men who did, but you're still upset. You feel guilty is what it is." Marcia begins to interrupt but he holds up a hand so she would let him finish.

"You feel guilty because you were about to answer the door but you asked her to do it instead. You feel guilty because when you came downstairs it was too late, she was already dead."

Tears form in her eyes.

"As she lay there dead on the floor, you couldn't go to her. You had to protect the children. You couldn't stay and go with her to the hospital or even comfort her mother in her time of need. That was the last time you saw her and you didn't even get a chance to say goodbye, did you?"

Marcia shakes her head. "I didn't even get a chance to

say goodbye," she whispers, salty tears lacing her quivering lips.

"Hon, look at me," he says as he lifts her chin. "It's not your fault. You couldn't do anything about it so you shouldn't be carrying all of this pain all of these years later. It's not your burden to bear. You should let it go. Let it go, Marcia...just say goodbye and let it go."

Terry wipes her face in the corner, trying not to disturb them as she sniffles behind her napkin. The pain this woman has endured for so long, the guilt she suffers from would kill her. How Marcia still remained sane after all of these years is a mystery, Terry thinks.

"But what about Cassius and Ruby?" she asks.

"What about them?"

"He wants to have the family he never had. He wants my baby."

"So why not let him?"

"Because...because..." she thinks aloud, "Even when we were together, he hardly saw Ruby. He never found the time for us." She feels her throat tighten and her eyes well up with tears again. "She never knew who her father was and he could've changed that but he didn't. Instead, all he did was take her away from everything that she and I had ever known. She doesn't know him, nor does she ask about him. It'll be too much of a shock for her. Besides, he loves this…more than he loved me or Ruby! And he's doing the same mess now that he did fifteen years ago! What makes now any different?"

"People change, Marci."

"But Jim, my relationship with my daughter suffers because of this. I've had to keep secrets from her and she probably doesn't trust me anymore. I can feel it! I…I know she doubts me. She questions me about things I can't answer and I can't deal with it anymore! I hate it! I can't tell her the truth and it hurts me!" She takes a deep breath and smooths her hair back.

"She's my best friend, my world, she's everything to me and the things that have happened in her past affect her today and she has no idea why!" She wipes her eyes and so does Terry from the opposite side of the room. Marcia is so focused on Jim's glassy eyes as she pours her heart out, admitting things to him that she couldn't even tell her husband. He seems saddened by it.

"Cassius is a selfish man and he's ruthless, Jim, and you know it."

He shakes his head slowly, processing what she's saying. He inhales deeply, sucking in a deep breath from the stem of his pipe. He exhales and reaches forward to dab her eyes again with his handkerchief.

"He has his flaws and no one can take that from him, but deep down inside he is a wonderful human being who is at war with himself because of the decisions *he's* made. He suffers from depression, Marci, the worst kind I've seen. He beats himself up every day because of what he's done to you, to your family." He pinches her cheeks. "I know you still love him, deep down inside, through all the pain, in your heart you still love him and guess what? He loves you too."

Terry's eyes widen as she forces herself to sit through the revealing details of Cassius' and Marcia's romantic past. She's heartbroken. Every word out of Marcia's mouth is confirmation that Cassius could never love her as much as he loves the woman who sits before her. She could never fill that empty void Marcia left in his heart, no matter how hard she tried. Cassius and Marcia had something that could never be duplicated. As much as Marcia tries to run from it, tries to deny it, she still holds onto the pain because deep down...

"I don't...I..."

"Don't fight it, woman!" Jim yells. He slams his frail hands on the table in front of him, sending the chess pieces flying everywhere but the board where they were meant to be.

"Everyone deserves a second chance! I'm not saying that the two of you should run off and leave the world behind you. What I'm saying is, you should learn to forgive him for all that he's done to you. Forgive him because trust me; it'll be harder to forgive yourself if you don't. He's already having a hard-enough time trying to get past the things he's done, believe me, I know. Been there, done that. He's got the weight of the world on his shoulders and now he's looking for answers. It will do him a lot of good if he knew that the woman he let get away, the woman who hated him so much, had finally found it in her heart to forgive him. He might find it in his heart to forgive himself. After all, he feels like he's done you more injustice than anyone else in the world and if you can learn to forgive, so can he."

As hard as it is, Marcia finally begins to see Jim's point. She looks at Terry, suddenly realizing she'd been there for the entire conversation. Terry's face shows the pain she feels but she manages to form a weak smile, and as Marcia opens her mouth to apologize, the office door swings wide open.

Sean and Cassius enter the room quickly and frantically. They're in mid-conversation when they realize they aren't alone.

"Terry, Marcia...what are you doing here?" Cassius says, in complete disbelief.

Terry glances between Marcia and Cassius, stunned. "I came here looking for you, and guess who I picked up along the way?"

Cassius stares angrily at Terry. She can't bear to look him in the eye.

"It's not her fault," Marcia continues. "She just told me where to start looking."

Cassius and Sean stand there dumbfounded, speechless. "Now, is there anyone in this room who can tell me where my daughter is?" Marcia says.

"Sean says Ruby is fine. Last he saw her was this morning and she was with Sheila," Cassius finally replies.

"Who the hell is Sean?"

"Sean, this is Marcia, Ruby's mother. Marcia, this is Sean, Ruby's...boyfriend."

"Boyfriend?!"

"Please, just listen to what he has to say, Marci. The people who were after Ruby are also after him. They took his brother instead. They're gonna kill him if we don't do something about it."

"WE?" Marcia jumps out of her chair. "I don't have to do nothin, once my child is here, we're leaving! I am not getting involved..."

Sean's head drops in defeat.

"Marcia, Sean saved Ruby's life. We owe it to him...to help him. He's a good kid, he just needs our help,"

Cassis pleads.

Marcia sizes him up but still isn't convinced.

"How do you know him Cassius, huh?"

He looks away, not wanting to answer.

"I asked you a QUESTION!" she snaps.

"He does a little side work for me but that's it...it's not what you think..."

"YOU SEE, he can't be a good kid if he's hanging around with you!"

"Marcia!" Jim shouts. "You should be ashamed of yourself! This boy saved your daughter's life," he says slowly. "He watched over her when her life was in danger and he loves her. Would you really turn your back on him now that you know how he feels about Ruby?"

"Jim, this is not my fight," she replies, calmer.

"Is it not? Are they not the same people who were after your daughter? Are they not the same people who were behind the killing of your friend Patricia? They are the *same,* girl, and it has always been your fight. It will continue to be your fight until they are dead!" Jim stands up and walks slowly to the other side of the table. He stands next to Sean and pats his chin.

"There was a time, when you hung around Cassius and so did your husband, but does that make you or him bad people?"

Marcia remains quiet, unable to say a thing. He's right and she's getting tired of him making his point.

"I didn't think so. Besides he was only a bookkeeper, I see no harm in that." Jim re-lights his pipe.

Marcia stares into Sean's eyes. There's a familiar look in them. There's pain, regret, but most importantly, there's love.

"I didn't mean to disrespect...I'm sorry," says Marcia.

Sean nods his head, accepting her apology. "Marcia, I tried to call Ruby a bunch of times but her phone is dead. Do you have Sheila's number so we can tell them to meet us here?"

"Yeah, I do." Marcia reaches into her bag and pulls out her cell phone. She dials Sheila's number and her niece picks up on the first ring.

"Aunt Marci, I was just about to call you!" Sheila sounds frantic. She's speaking so fast.

"Sheila, I...I can't hear you! What are you saying?"

"It's ok, baby, it's ok...you're not bleeding, just hold on for me..."

"SHEILA! Who are you talking to? What's going on? Where's Ruby?"

"They took her, they took her!" Sheila screams.

"What do you mean they TOOK HER?" Marcia yells into the phone. Everyone else in the room falls quiet, holding their breath, waiting to hear more. Marcia put Sheila on speaker phone after Cassius' request.

"She ran away from us because we were gonna take her home," she screams breathlessly into her headset. Sheila speeds through town desperately searching for the nearest hospital and even though David isn't covered in blood, she's afraid of internal bleeding. The bruising on his chest is unlike anything she's ever seen before. He's in so much pain.

"...and my friend David went back to my house to see if she went back there and he found her, but they were there waiting for her! They shot him twice and took her away in a black Honda!"

"What did they look like, Sheila? What did they look like?"

"Black hoodies. They always wear black hoodies, right? The men who killed your friend were wearing black hoodies?"

Marcia almost dropped the phone, Cassius and Jim looked like they had seen a ghost.

"How do you know about that? How..."

"It doesn't matter right now, Aunt Marci, but I have a message for Ruby's father. Will you be able to give this to

246

him?"

Marcia looks at Cassius, stunned that Sheila knows as much as she does.

"Yeah, go ahead..."

"The same man that was behind his failed assassination fifteen years ago is the same man that kidnapped Ruby. Fortunately, Mike works for him and he told me everything this man has been planning to do to overthrow Ruby's father. He's plotting to kill him, Ruby, and Sean."

"What's his name?" Cassius sneers.

Sheila hesitates.

"Who is this?"

"WHAT IS HIS NAME?" he barks.

"Tony. Mike said his name is Tony, a white guy from the Bronx."

Cassius' stomach drops. He falls back into a nearby chair to catch his breath. Terry runs over to him with a glass of water, fanning him with a piece of paper, hoping that it'll help, but it doesn't.

It was *my fault,* he thinks. *I put my own daughter in danger without even knowing it! How could I be so careless? Why did I hold that meeting with them? I should've just handled it myself. I basically shoved her picture in their faces and told them where to look!*

"Sheila, meet me at the gym on Linden now. You know where that is?"

"Yeah, I'll be there after I drop David off at the hospital."

Marcia hangs up, furious. She turns to Cassius, ready to unleash hell and fury on him, but she stops. His face…she never realized how much their daughter looks like him, and all over his face is pain and suffering. Jim was right. This isn't all his fault. She forced Jerome to call Cassius in the first place.

Jerome always told her to let up and stop being so overprotective of the girl, but she couldn't help it. He tried to tell her again, weeks ago, and even though she agreed to it, she still didn't listen. Now she's sitting in Jim's Gym, surrounded by old memories and an incomprehensible fear that she will never see her daughter alive again.

The truth is, throughout her early adulthood and even now, she used her daughter as comfort. When she was separated from her family, she always had her baby girl. And when Jerome left for months on end, she still had her precious Ruby. The nightmares she relived about Patricia's death used to haunt her night after night, sending her running into her daughter's room and snuggling up next to her. The guilt she felt about being with Jerome, the father of Patricia's child, was justified by Ruby's presence. She fell in love with him by default. Although, they had a strong friendship beforehand, she never felt the same way about him like how she felt for Cassius. She could never be with the man she truly loved and the closest she would ever get to him was through the miracle they created together, Ruby.

Ruby was the only thing that kept her sane throughout the years. But, when Ruby left home a few weeks ago, she felt her life start to unravel. She began to have horrible thoughts and the nightmares returned. She behaved out of character, or was her true character emerging from a deep slumber, she wonders? The only way to fix it was to find Ruby and bring her home. But she's afraid. Afraid of what she might do if something ever happened to her child.

Marcia watches as Terry tries her best to comfort Cassius but he seems not to be listening to her. Marcia looks at her phone again and sees twenty missed calls from Jerome! Had she been so out of it that she didn't hear her phone ringing?

"I have to call Jerome back. I've missed every last one of his calls today!"

Cassius wipes his forehead with a napkin Terry handed him.

"Yes, please…tell him to come now. If we're going to take Tony down, we'll need to do it together and right now, I don't trust anyone else other than your family and the people in this room."

Cassius approaches Marcia and grabs her hands in his. "I'm sorry I didn't listen to you when you suspected the attack came from within, Marcia. This is my fault and I will make it right. We'll take him down, together."

"I'm not the same woman I was all those years ago, Cassius," Marcia stares deep into his troubled eyes. They're dark and regretful, yet strong. Adrenaline rises within her chest again and her breaths are quick and short.

"I'm not the same man I was either. I'll die before I let anything happen to our daughter, to you. The entire city will burn if it has to and Tony with it. When I get through with him for ruining our family…he'll wish for a swift death, and I won't give it to him."

Marcia collapses her head into his chest as he draws her into his embrace. Her body shivers with rage. Her sobs are muffled in his arms and there is nothing anyone in the room can do to comfort her.

"Cassius…" she says after a moment.

"Yes?"

"When you kill him, I want to be there. I want to see the life leave his cold eyes and curse his spirit as it descends to hell. And if I find out that he has touched my daughter in any way, I will murder him myself."

"I know you will, Marcia," replies Cassius. "I know you will."

Chapter 17

Ruby is tossed onto her face and onto a cold damp floor covered in plastic. The far corner of the room is dark, pitch black. She couldn't make out much of anything once they pulled the blindfold off. There's something on the other side of the room where the light fades and darkness begins, but she can't identify what it is.

Her head aches and the spot where she was hit throbs unlike anything she's felt before. If only she could free her hands. She struggles but there's no use. The plastic zip ties are cutting into her wrists, each movement cuts deeper into her flesh. Her eyes adjust to the light. Four men stand before her, talking amongst themselves.

"What do you want me to do with her?"

"I don't know, what do *you* think we should do with her?" a barefoot man replies.

Her heart beats faster.

Do with me?

"She looks like a good piece of meat to me," says the one who attacked her in the street. Her eyes widen with disbelief as she realizes…

He's the man from the bus!

Tony smiles and winks at her.

"Yeah, she looks real pretty, just like that fine mother of hers."

"So, what you wanna do?" asks Hakim.

"I always wondered if her mother was a good lay," Tony replies as he undoes his belt. "Let's see how far that apple fell from the tree."

Ruby's vision fades to black as images from her life flash before her. At every obstacle, every difficult moment in her life, her mother was always there. She protected her like a fierce lioness, but...she's not here. Not now. She's alone, afraid. Her lack of faith in her mother drove her here and now, she's about to suffer greatly for it.

These men are going to kill me and...I'll never see her again.

A veil of darkness closes in tight on a memory of her five-year-old self cuddling with her mother in bed, resting safe in her arms. Tears stream down her face as she succumbs to the horror that has finally settled in.

Mommy...

BLOOD OF A QUEEN TRILOGY: CHARACTER BIOS

Learn more about Ruby and the other characters in the *Blood of a Queen* Trilogy.

Name: Ruby Matthews

Nickname: Rube

Age: 21

Gender: Female

Ethnicity: African American

Body Type: Athletic

Occupation: Student

Marital Status: Single

Education: College

Character Type: Protagonist

Back Story:

An overly sheltered young woman named Ruby is finally granted the freedom she'd been yearning for all her life. Drawn to the very place her mother and stepfather dedicated their lives to protect her from, Ruby heads to New York City. Unbeknownst to her, Ruby's arrival resets the wheels in motion to overthrow a troubled yet powerful Kingpin. During her quest, she encounters a forbidden love interest and she struggles between following her young heart or remaining loyal to a long-lost childhood friend.

Goal:

With the help of her cousin Sheila, Ruby plans to uncover the truth and prove the innocence of the very people who have kept it from her.

Name: Marcia Matthews-Greene

Nickname: Ce Ce

Age: 41

Gender: Female

Ethnicity: African American

Body Type: Pear shaped

Occupation: Celebrity designer

Marital Status: Married

Education: Some college

Relation to Main Character: Mother

Backstory:

Marcia, Ruby's mother and notable celebrity designer, struggles to keep her wits as her daughter secretly sets out to uncover the truth behind a dark family secret she'd hoped to leave in the past. Every misstep and rebellious act from Ruby drives Marcia into further uncertainty and panic, unraveling the life she has built to protect her daughter at all costs.

Goal:

Before Ruby gets too close to the truth, Marcia must convince her to come home before their enemies find her first.

Name: Jerome Greene
Nickname: Jerry/JT
Age: 44
Gender: Male
Ethnicity: African American
Body Type: Athletic/Tall
Occupation: Oncologist
Marital Status: Married
Education: Ph.D.
Relation to Main Character: Stepfather

Backstory:

Jerome, Ruby's stepfather, is Ruby's biggest advocate for her freedom and independence. He convinced Marcia to allow their daughter to grow into the beautiful young woman they've raised her to be. But he grows eerily suspicious when Ruby runs to New York and disappears after a family dispute.

Goal:

Jerome must keep the peace between him and his wife while trying to figure out what Ruby is truly up to.

Name: Sheila Matthews

Nickname: Shells

Age: 25

Gender: Female

Ethnicity: African American

Body Type: Hourglass

Occupation: Law student/volunteer/domestic violence advocate

Marital Status: Single

Education: B.A.

Relation to Main Character: Cousin

Backstory:

Ruby's cousin Sheila joins her to solve a mystery that haunts their family. Sheila recruits the help of a police captain, David, to help solve the fifteen-year-old cold case. With a painful history of her own, Sheila realizes Ruby's mystery is similar to another cold case she's been working on. Ruby's troubled past may very well lead to the answers she's been looking for.

Goal:

Unexpected obstacles stand in their way at every turn and Sheila must help Ruby crack this cold case, maintain Ruby's trust, and keep her out of danger along the way.

Name: Pamela Brown
Nickname: Pam
Age: 20
Gender: Female
Ethnicity: African American
Body Type: Angular/Pregnant
Occupation: Retail associate
Marital Status: Complicated
Education: Working on GED
Relation to Main Character: Childhood friend

Backstory:

Ruby reunites with her childhood friend, Pam, whom she'd lost touch with fifteen years earlier. Secret about her true intentions, Pam is embraced by Ruby, who is excited to reignite their long-lost friendship. The absence of Pam's mother reveals a dark secret. Overwhelmed with disbelief, Ruby sets forth to uncover the truth for herself.

Goal:

Pam wants to avenge her mother's death and make those responsible pay for it. There are at least two people who were present on that fateful night and she won't rest until she knows the truth.

Name: Michael Matthews

Nickname: Mike

Age: 26

Gender: Male

Ethnicity: African American

Body Type: Thin and tall

Occupation: "Piece" in underground drug ring

Marital Status: Single

Education: Some college

Relation to Main Character: Cousin

Backstory:

Mike, a close cousin of Ruby and Sheila, is down on his luck when he stumbles upon the opportunity of a lifetime. Too ambitious for his own good, he enlists with a top "Player" in a drug ring who promises fortune beyond Mike's wildest dreams. His new boss, Tony, keeps dangerous company within the ranks, but the longer Mike sticks around, the more he realizes Tony could possibly be the most dangerous of them all.

Goal:

Mike yearns to be more independent and less reliant upon Sheila's financial assistance. When his golden opportunity proves to be more dangerous than he anticipated, he must choose between his luxury lifestyle and his curious family.

Name: Sean
Nickname: None
Age: 26
Gender: Male
Ethnicity: African American
Body Type: Medium Height/Weight
Occupation: Warehouse worker
Marital Status: Complicated
Education: High school diploma
Relation to Main Character: Protector/Love interest

Backstory:

Sean, a young man with big dreams, struggles to avoid the street lifestyle that has consumed his community. Angry with life and fed up with his ex-girlfriend Pam, Sean takes to the punching bags at Jim's Gym, where he meets a man who will change his life forever. With a seemingly innocent agreement, the two form an unlikely bond that will be challenged in the days to come.

Goal:

Sean wants to leave his hometown in search for a better life, to attend college, and to settle down with someone who is worthy of his heart. A simple assignment from his mentor may offer a quick solution to allow him to follow his dreams—that is, if he can make it out alive.

Name: Cassius
Nickname: Scully
Age: 46
Gender: Male
Ethnicity: African American
Body Type: Tall/Stocky
Occupation: Kingpin
Marital Status: Complicated
Education: None
Relation to Main Character: Unknown

Backstory:

Cassius, also known as Scully, is the powerful Kingpin of New York City. He inherited a fading drug empire many years ago and grew it to new heights. Cassius utilizes chess tactics and strategies to wage war on the city in an effort to gain complete control, and designates the key players in each borough as "Pieces." The Pieces play an important role in his empire—the Queen being the one he prizes most.

Goal:

Weary from years of sexual affairs, drug smuggling, and blackmailing corrupt politicians, Cassius yearns for freedom and forgiveness. Not a man of many regrets, there is only one decision he can no longer live with: the unforgivable sacrifice he's made to protect his empire.

Name: Tony

Nickname: None

Age: 40

Gender: Male

Ethnicity: European/Italian

Body Type: Short/Stocky

Occupation: "Player" in drug ring

Marital Status: Married

Education: High school diploma

Relation to Main Character: Unknown

Backstory:

Tony, Mike's boss and a head "Player" under Scully's regime, has spent much of his life living in Scully's shadow. While seemingly content with his position, Tony trains Mike along with a group of men called "Pieces" to run his regions of the Bronx as he sets his sights higher and makes his team stronger.

Goal:

Sensing that Scully's regime may be weakened, Tony focuses his efforts on making his men more powerful than their colleagues in neighboring boroughs. With Mike, his protégé in training, Tony prepares to make his strongest power move yet.

ABOUT THE AUTHOR

Toi Powell

A KING'S RANSOM:
The second novel in the *Blood of a Queen* Trilogy

By day, Toi Powell lives a double life like that of secret spy working in digital advertising in New York City. Yet, under the cloak of night, she writes thrilling tales of hidden secrets, forbidden love, and family dramatics through robust characters. Ten years after finishing the initial manuscript of her first trilogy, *Blood of a Queen*, she no longer allowed self-doubt to determine her destiny. *Blood of a Queen: Book 1* was self-published in 2016 with the second book in the trilogy, *A King's Ransom*, soon to follow.

Her goal is to encourage and motivate others who stand in their own way of achieving greatness. She resides in New Jersey, never too far from close friends and her loving family.

POST A RATING/LEAVE A COMMENT OR REVIEW

If you enjoyed reading the second book of this trilogy and would like to see it continue, please visit Amazon.com to post a star rating and short comment to let the author and others know what you thought about *A King's Ransom: The second novel in the Blood of a Queen trilogy*.

In less than five seconds, you can help spread the word about this book, and the author by posting a review which is critical for independent authors like Toi Powell. She can't do this without your help and support. Amazon awaits!

SHARE WITH YOUR BOOK CLUBS

Share *A King's Ransom* with members of your book club. Contact the author if you'd like to set up a social Q&A for any questions, interviews or behind the scenes information on characters not found in the book. Toi loves interacting with her readers!

KEEP IN TOUCH WITH THE AUTHOR

Toi can't wait to speak with you! Follow her on the social media platforms below and tell her how much you loved the book! Also, visit *ToiPowell.com* to join the mailing list for updates and upcoming books.

WEBSITES:
Author Site: ToiPowell.com
Blog Site: TheToiHouse.com

SOCIAL MEDIA:
Goodreads: Goodreads.com/toistori
YouTube: Toicollection
Twitter: TheToiHouse
Instagram: TheToiHouse/ToiPowell
Facebook.com/TheToiHouse
Pinterest: ToiHouse

Download the music
BLOOD OF A QUEEN
Performed by Toi Powell

Available at the following locations:
iTunes, Apple Music, Google Play,
Amazon mp3, Tidal

TOI POWELL